Why me?

By Tony Hurley

Published by
Chipmunkapublishing
PO Box 6872
Brentwood
Essex
CM13 1ZT

Copyright   © 2004 Chipmunkapublishing

A record of this book is in the British Library
ISBN 190469702X

Printed and bound in Great Britain

Preface

It is a privilege to have this opportunity to pay tribute to Tony. I have worked with the Open University for over 20 years and have met some remarkable people in the course of my work. Tony is one of the most remarkable. I know that his story will be an inspiration to all who read it.

Any one of the tremendous challenges that Tony has faced throughout his life might have crushed the spirit of most people, and could well have crushed his. Unbelievably, however, he has faced them all with courage, determination and humour and still has the energy to tell his tale. This is all the more unbelievable when one appreciates that his difficulties did not follow on conveniently, one from another, but weaved their wicked paths in amongst each other, throughout Tony's life, often overlapping in their devastation.

It would not have been obvious to me, had I not grown to know Tony over his years as an Open University student, that he had such a battle on his hands. He has been an example to us all in the way he has struggled on with his studies despite all his difficulties. Some years he had to put the studies aside, some years he had to be content with a worse result than he knew he was capable of, but he would always bounce back into the next course with enthusiasm, modesty and gratitude.

Tony's regular expressions of gratitude have been for me one of the most humbling aspects of my relationship with him. It would be so easy to become demanding, bitter, complaining and miserable in the face of such an unfair share of life-difficulties. Tony never has. His exemplary spirit has been an inspiration to me. For this, I thank him most sincerely.

Chris Youle, Senior Counsellor, the Open University.

1. Introduction

My reason for writing this account of my experience of manic depression is that it may help other's who suffer from this illness. It may also help those, whose lives have not been touched by it, to understand the stress and the bad feelings associated with this traumatic condition.

Because it appertains to the mind and is not manifested physically, people have difficulty in dealing with it. A sufferer needs understanding and patience above all else. The sufferer cannot put a bandage around his depression or around an elated mood. Both of these terrible states are hell for the manic-depressive. In order to give some perspective into its bipolar nature, manic depression has two phases; one up and one down. The down phase is a severe depression that can deprive a person of reason and lead to a drastic end - suicide.

We all suffer from depression, but the depression associated with manic depression leaves the sufferer like a piece of blotting paper. No energy, no motivation, not wanting to see anyone, not wanting to eat, just wanting to stay in bed all day. The high state also can have far-reaching effects and be very dramatic, with the ill person bearing the consequences. For example, he or she feels on top of the world, and might go off with credit cards and spend a lot of money that they do not have. They could also get into all sorts of relationships.

Manic depression could also have a correlation with alcoholism, and sufferers could find themselves eventually in prison. My drinking covered up my manic state; my friends associated it with my being gregarious - actually, I was inebriated. I was once arrested and jailed mistakenly for being drunk, which only worsened the trauma. This I will describe in more detail later. Even though the illness is bipolar, a person may experience only one phase. The illness is now called bipolar affective disorder and even though this is an improvement on 'manic depression', it is still quite a mouthful.

Manic depression has always carried with it a bad image. This applies to both the condition and those whose mental health is affected by it - people are scared of it. Therefore, in future I will refer to the condition as bi-polar disorder, or 'mood swings', which is exactly what it is.

Another reference I will make is in relation to the partner, who will be called the carer. This could be a relation, friend etc. This person has to be of a certain calibre because he or she has a very difficult undertaking and role. Personally, I have been lucky enough to have aides who look out for me.

I would like to dedicate this book to a very special friend of mine, Eamon Coyne, who died fourteen years ago. He was instrumental in my motivation to write this book. During his life, he encouraged me to put my experiences down on paper, so that they might be of benefit to others. With that sincere advice in mind, it will please me if my writing is of help to another.

At the time, I began to think about writing an autobiography it was no big deal, but I felt that if it would help someone, then it would be a good thing to do. I discussed this idea with my psychiatrist and GP a few times. It sometimes seemed like one of those grandiose ideas that were not produced by a rational mind; being a mood swinger, I can see an idea as being legitimate, when to anyone else it is hare-brained.

I carried out some research in the library trying to find somewhere I could learn to write as I was groping in the dark. I did find out what was required to publish a book, through lists of publishers, details of costs and the vanity publishers. From newspapers and magazines, I was able to get helpful hints and details of writing groups, which were not too expensive to attend.

At the very least I felt that researching this book, and looking at the possibilities of some further study courses, would take up the greater part of an otherwise undedicated year. At best, it would help to maintain stability in my mental state. I was glad that I had gotten over a high I had been experiencing - one that did not last long and which I thought I had handled well.

I have mentioned before, there is the time leading up to a high and the coming down, both of which have to be dealt with. I feel sad and cheated that all of the times associated with these bouts of mood swings seem to have taken years from my life. The arthritis I suffer from I feel is more 'legitimate' - it is an illness that society accepts. I feel guilty about being a mood swinger. Should I have been given a choice I would rather any illness than this. I become preoccupied with such thoughts when I am not engaged in studies or constructive activities.

2. Early Years and First Experiences

I had better go back to the beginning, to my childhood. At the age of about seven years, I had great difficulty sleeping and used to creep into my parents' bed at night. Not being able to sleep was most frustrating. At this time, I also became very scrupulous about my religion - I was a Roman Catholic. I would repeat a prayer up to ten times before I was satisfied I had said it correctly. In the home, locking doors and turning off lights would be checked repeatedly. This early sign of the obsessive perfectionist is another trait of mood swings, although the observation results from reflection.

These traits lasted until I was about fifteen years old, but the remnants are still with me. Apart from these lapses, I grew up on a par with boys of my age. My parents were ordinary working class people with three children - my sister, my brother and myself.

At the age I am describing, times were difficult in Ireland. It was just after the Second World War, and food and money were scarce. I went to a National School, which was of a very poor standard, I am sorry to say. From National School, I graduated to Technical School. This was based on a manual rather than an academic education. My technical education cost 25 shillings a year, but after the first year at the School, I obtained a scholarship. This was followed by two courses that cost 12/6 each.

Today, the Technical School has been replaced by an advanced place of education, which combines secondary education, grammar school and technical teaching. It seemed at the time that to send me to secondary school would have taken me along a route that might lead to university. This would have been too expensive for my parents, and in any event, at that stage, university was pie in the sky for me. I regarded rich people as being the only ones able to avail them of

8

such a luxury as education, even though I have always known that if I had expressed this as my desire, my parents would have found the money to fund it - somehow.

I began work when I was seventeen years old. One year later, I moved to another job at a mill - life was normal and I was enjoying myself. The mill manager and I worked in harmony. He often suggested to me that I was destined for greater things. Eventually, he took over the post of commercial traveller, selling our products throughout six counties.

For a period of twelve months, I took care of the organisation of the mill, as well as my own designated clerical work, and deputised for the commercial traveller when necessary. Travelling around the countryside appealed to me. As I did not drive, a chauffeur accompanied me. Then at the age of twenty came my first real brush with depression; I had had some minor episodes before, but this was a real knock out.

At the beginning of the episode, I refused to get out of bed; I did not want to see anyone. My poor mother was so bewildered and upset that she found it difficult to cope at all. A personnel officer from the mill came to see me and reported to my managing director, who in turn then sent for my mother. He suggested that if she could get me to see his own doctor, help might be at hand. As I had great respect for my managing director, I went to see his doctor, who advised me to go to a mental hospital in the nearest city - Cork.

I should explain that my hometown was small - its population around 2000 - and it was approximately 30 miles from Cork. As with all small towns, everyone knows everyone else's business. Back in the 1950s, there was no television, and we hardly knew what The Financial Times was. Local gossip was the main source of news, not necessarily malicious, but as I became the main topic, it was difficult to swallow.

9

The news of my dilemma got out and my case turned out to be a major drama: the stigma of mental illness condemned me. My family drew up a plan - I should go to stay with my aunt in a town called Kinsale, supposedly for a holiday. Kinsale was 20 miles from my hometown. My brother took me to a hospital in Cork for treatment as a day patient on Tuesdays. I was treated in the morning with electro-convulsion therapy (ECT). This consisted of the patient, under anaesthetic, receiving a shot of electricity in his or her brain.

Briefly, what happened was as follows: the anaesthetic was administered, electrodes were attached to both temples and the shock emitted. I cannot remember for sure, but I recall being strapped to my bed as the convulsion reverberated around my body. I awoke with an almighty headache, but otherwise OK. My brother came to collect me in the late afternoon and normal life resumed. I felt better because of the treatment and was prepared to continue with it, even though I was scared of the hospital and its unfamiliar surroundings.

Picture one of those old movies where they are taking a prisoner into a weird building to subject him to torture - this was happening to me, only it was for real, and meant to be for my own good. A second visit took place the following Thursday, and after both treatments I was feeling good. In fact, it seemed to me as though nothing had been wrong.

After a week's 'holiday', I returned to my hometown and to work. I could not understand the transformation in myself - it felt great to be back in the real world. I felt rather puzzled by my swift change of moods. It was a contradiction in terms: everything had changed and yet nothing had changed. It is difficult to explain such a good feeling and the devastation of the reverse. The depression you experience under mood swings wipes you to the floor and prevents you from getting up.

Returning to the episode described above, it appeared that no one had heard of my ordeal. Had anything leaked out, I would not have been able to cope with the embarrassment. One thing I did learn and appreciate was the support I received from my managing director. As the years go by, I continue to acknowledge what a wonderful man he was. I was due for promotion at the time of my breakdown, which was subsequently postponed.

A year later, I was promoted - from accounts manager to mill manager. This entailed being in charge of about 60 employees manufacturing animal foodstuffs, and in the process supplying six counties' farmers with work. The managing directors were the powerful figures driving the wheel and I enjoyed a good working relationship with them, as I did with the mill workers.

Then came change - a director from a subsidiary firm came to our mill and took over as the main man in charge of operations. Neither my managing director nor I could get on with him. A year later, I left, as I was no longer happy there and my managing director had died.

Being unhappy was an understatement. Months before I resigned, I had become terribly depressed and could not tell anyone about my condition. At that stage, I was ignorant of what was happening to me - what I did know was that it was difficult to cope with the depression and it only added to my misery to not be able to confide in my family or friends.

Having left my job, the situation seemed to improve and I felt a little better. I had always felt I did not want to leave my parental home, but that change too would come sooner rather than later, as I made up my mind I could support them just as well if I went away. The reasons for my change of mind were numerous - my father was not well, my brother and sister had already left home - was it right for me to leave now?

3. Friends and Relationships

It was 1967, London, and there were parties every weekend; a good time was had by all. During this period I had a nice girlfriend who was good company and easy to get along with. I struck up a great rapport with her friends as well. Not because it suited me, rather for her sake I went to the pub with her to have a few drinks. She enjoyed a hot toddy; the recipe consisted of a shot of whisky, honey, cloves and hot water. You can imagine that it was a lot to mix together, and the barmen then did not want the trouble. Nowadays it's a regular drink attracting no more fuss than any other cocktail.

June, my girlfriend, used to accompany me to parties, where I did my usual thing - out to the back room with the boys to drink and enjoy a singsong. She did not seem to mind, or at least, did not complain. My friends pointed out on a number of occasions that was not the way to treat a lady. I did not intend to be disrespectful to any of my girlfriends - on the contrary, I meant them to have a good time. It was like having a couple of personalities, but what I did not realise was the problem it created for others around me.

It was rather difficult for others, and for me, to cope with the uncertainty of what temperament I might be in. There was the additional agony of finding out that maybe I had appeared to be arrogant (unintentionally and unknowingly) to someone, and to not have a single recollection of it. I have also learned that mood swingers are inclined to put themselves down and see themselves in bad light. In other words, they are not able to love themselves.

The stigma attached to mental illness has always caused me grave worry. I was afraid that the nature of my illness would betray me. So many are ignorant of their mental disorder and this puts them at a major disadvantage. In my own case, I am writing this account with the benefit of hindsight.

On at least two occasions, I took June home from parties just in time for her to get ready to go to work - she was a nurse. We dated for nearly a year and then things came to an abrupt end. To this day, I am unable to figure out what brought about such a swift rift - I could not contact her or her friends. I became very frustrated as June and her friends were nice people. I could not understand their tactics when I tried to get in touch, like having the phone slam down on me.

I could not recall anything that I could have done or said to cause such a situation to arise - at least as far as I could remember. I had not told anyone about my disorder; maybe June had heard I had been in a mental hospital. Yet I thought her too understanding to have put me down because of that. I knew she was planning to go to Canada for a year anyhow, so I gave up the ghost.

Without knowing it, I was a little high at the time. Anyway, if there was anything wrong with me, I thought my friends would have told me. In recalling the relationship with June, something stuck in my mind, albeit trivial. One night, the husband of her best friend mentioned to me that it was about time June and I married. I retorted jokingly that maybe he fancied her himself. This conversation took place shortly before our break-up, and I racked my brains to recall any other misdemeanour on my part. I simply could not figure out what had caused the abrupt end. Silence seemed a nasty way of rebuking someone whom you had seemingly cared for, and I would have stood constructive criticism no matter my state of mind.

There is little consolation in the saying 'there's naught as queer as folk'. June went off to Canada, and was away for twelve months. Upon her return, I tried to get in touch with her, and finally managed to speak to her best friend, Jenny. She said, 'Do you know who is here with me? June.' Then the phone went dead. Even though I was still very upset, I decided this had to be the grand finale.

I thought that life was going swimmingly and would continue to do so. Work was enjoyable and it had a good social side. I played football with the firm's team, and it was good fun once a week. We held a successful record against other business teams. The girls from the office followed the team, which meant there were many parties after the games. I was playing badminton regularly at a club in Kings Cross.

I had met a girl who was worked in Victoria near to where my job was based. We became very good friends and derived tremendous enjoyment from each other's company. My trouble was that, being mentally ill, I could never allow myself to get too involved with a female partner. There was no point in kidding myself; I was different from everyone else.

It was around this time that I got to know an elderly couple who lived in South Kensington - Pierce and Louise McCann. They were to become very special friends of mine. Pierce was a big character, and Louise was gentle and holy. Louise knew all about mood swings. She was one of the few people that I confided in and who understood me. The one exception she took to my life-style was that she thought I should be married - she even made matches for me.

By Louise's books, I could do no wrong. I am glad that, for a period of nearly twenty years, I took Louise to church each week and afterwards often to a park. The priest and most of the congregation of the parish church thought she was my mother. Any time I was not available to participate in this outing, I would get Eamon Coyne to substitute for me. We two had a mutual friend, Sean Fitzsimons, and I think that Pierce and Louise regarded us three as their sons.

Again, I must say that things *seemed* just great and I was full of energy and confidence. I remember I used to pop into the office of the girlfriend I was dating, Carol, completely unannounced. Irrespective of who was there with her, I would carry on laughing and joking; poor Carol must have been mortified.

Then suddenly, I was no longer bright and cheerful but the opposite, feeling miserable and thinking that no one was taking notice of my change of mood, or seeing anything different in me. Gradually, I withdrew socially and hated it when my friends come around to invite me out. When they mentioned that I was very quiet, it mad me wish that I could be Houdini and disappear. I struggled on in this way for a couple of months getting even more depressed.

One thing that I would like to say is that, as I look back upon this unhappy period, I cannot find the words to describe how wonderful my friends have been. Ironically, at the time, I could not respond to their care and concern. I could not raise myself from the depression and its killer effects.

1976
I was frightened by the prospect of a relationship as I felt that having mental problems would be a deterrent. I would not wish to saddle anyone else with my cross; it was mine to bear alone. Another reason was that if I had children, would they be affected? I had to accept life was going to sell me a bit short. I would have to rise to the challenge given to me, and perhaps God would provide compensation in other ways.

1978
Nineteen seventy-eight was a very good year or at least, life was good to me. Some of my friends had left London, but one good friend, Eamon Coyne, remained on hand. He had a wonderful disposition and was a marvellous confidante. He was endowed with a hugely understanding and charitable nature, and was always helping people in need. With my crutches; the lithium,

the visits to the hospital and friends to confide in, especially Eamon, I had no real troubles.

In September, there was an event that went unnoticed by me at the time. It is with hindsight that I recognise its significance. I went on a holiday to America with Sean, another very good friend of mine. We toured from the West Coast right across to the East Coast. The first night we spent in San Francisco, I could not sleep and was out of bed at 3 am. When morning came, Sean could not find me. He looked inside a small room to find me reading and asked if I was ok. I reassured him nothing was wrong except I was unable to sleep.

A couple of sleepless nights later, I decided to go for a walk, again at around 3am. I did not know where I was, and it turned out to be a rundown area - not a safe place to be at that time of night, on one's own. In the morning, I explained to others in the hotel where I had wandered, they told me I had been in an area called the 'Joint', which had a reputation for low life.

Throughout the three-week vacation these sleepless nights continued. I did not know then that sleeplessness is a manifestation of the manic phase. I recall that I was argumentative during our US trip, and one night in Arizona, Sean got annoyed with my manner. However, we did not fall out. This arrogance and argumentativeness are also manifestations of the high mood. By the time we returned to England, I was in better form and sleeping well again.

The 1980's passed without incident. Life in general was fulfilling - my social life was good and I was enjoying myself. When I was on good form, as was then the case, I really relished my work. It had now been three years since I had last been hospitalised and I was secretly very proud of that. There were times when I was noticeably depressed and anxious, but these were minor blips, and my visits to the hospital were able to resolve these difficult times.

Socially, life was quiet. I was not drinking, and my friends were constantly in touch and as helpful as ever. It was so difficult for both them and me. When I was depressed, I wanted to be on my own. Whilst my friends wanted to help, they did not want to be intrusive. As I have mentioned before, it was a barbed wire entanglement of a situation. At work I was OK, although maybe a little timid. Both with work and with friends, I harbour a great fear that people will discover my mental problem and use it against me.

Some of my friends know something is fundamentally wrong with me, and I think that out of protective feelings towards me, they would prefer not to get to the bottom of this flaw. They would rather that I retain my privacy and pain, and support me as best they can. My good friend Eamon was my tower of strength, although even this falls infinitely short of the esteem that I hold as regards to him. The best tribute I could bestow is that that he was like a father and a mother to me. All tried to help, but it was Eamon's support that meant the most to me throughout our friendship.

I had known Eamon since 1967, and sometimes I wondered if he spent more time with me than with his wife. He had been introduced to me by a friend, Hugh O'Donnell, who had collected me from Shenley Hospital after a stay there. He had asked Eamon if he would take me into his home and give me temporary accommodation. He was always there when I needed him, and always ready to help me. He really tried to understand my psyche and, more than anyone else, I would accept his advice and encouragement. He was a great listener and, from my point of view, that was highly important. Of course, I refrained from encroaching on his goodness, but if I did, he had great patience as well.

I met up with a friend, Denis Treacy, and he mentioned to me that I did not look well. I had known him for at least twenty-five years, but had never told him about my mood swings. I decided to tell him then, and he suggested that we went to his flat and had a proper talk. It proved to be a wonderful conversation, and him to be a person of great understanding. More of this will become evident later on.

1989

A few more months passed and Eamon, my lifelong good friend, died suddenly. This was a terrible blow; it was as if my whole world had fallen apart. How would I manage without him, the one person in this world who understood me? It was a huge loss, especially as it was so completely unexpected - he was just forty-five years old. For a couple of days, it was as if I was in a trance. How was I going to live without him? Eamon had been my prop over so many years.

However, I thought I had a few good things going for me. It was now fifteen years since I had been in a mental hospital and, as far as I was concerned, that was some achievement. With the ongoing help of the psychiatric unit and The Manic Depression Fellowship (more of which later), I had learned a lot about my mental state. Although I had begun to suffer with Arthritis, the Rheumatology department at the hospital was taking care of this. I had also begun to study at the Open University and this had proved to be very therapeutic to me. These elements of my life will be mentioned in more detail later.

Eamon was the one who had encouraged me in the first instance to write all of this down. These thoughts seemed to lift my spirits and the sadness and gloom dispersed. The consultant psychiatrist at the West Middlesex Hospital was very attentive to me during the months after Eamon's death.

At this time I used to visit my friend Denis Treacy, seeing him once or twice a week and really appreciating being able to talk to him. He was someone who understood me. I would often say to him 'if I am boring, shut me up'. Denis would read my assignments for the Open University and always gave me great encouragement. I think that others' reassurance has been very important for my studies. He was a great pal to talk to. It seemed as if he knew all about mood swings, yet he said he knew only what I had told him. Once he did know, he could remember times when I had seemed a bit peculiar in the past, but as I was also drinking at those times, he had put it down to that. I have often thought that if there were more people as understanding as Denis, Paul and Clarice, it would have made my life much easier.

1993
It was now summer. One evening, I was on my way to visit my friends Paul and Clarice. I had never told them that I was mood swinger, and had been wondering for some time if I should. This is a situation that normal people do not have to confront. For me, it was an agonising decision. If I did not tell them, nothing would happen; to disclose my condition could prompt a distressing response.

On the one hand I do want to be honest with my friends, but by being honest, will some people find it hard to understand what mood swings are? For many, a conversation about mental illness is taboo. Anybody affected by mood swings will confirm that, to some people, we are like the beast from ten thousand fathoms deep! Maybe I am overstating it, but life can be a lonely place. On the other hand, there are people who do understand, and this improves our situation so much. In the end, I decided to tell Paul and Clarice about my illness, and thank goodness that they understood. We became closer friends as a result, and my fears about what might have been were allayed.

4. The Self Destructive Impulse

The First Attempt - 1964

Early one morning, I decided to gas myself. I just could not bear the weight of my depression any longer. Some people say suicide is an easy way out, others a cry for help. I think it is neither when I feel that low - there is nowhere to go, and nowhere is free of my misery. This is the floor, I am lying on it and I cannot get up. Any logic disappears. There is only one way out.

Even today, the word suicide sticks in my throat. After my first attempt at suicide, I recall waking up in bed in Edgware General Hospital. Oxygen masks were all around, and I was but semi-conscious. The trauma of coming to terms with the whole episode came next. Being a Roman Catholic made it even more a matter of personal conscience and guilt, particularly at that time. As I lay there, all I could think of was what a coward I was. I could not even entertain the word suicide.

I had a few visitors, but their visits made me feel worse. After several weeks, I returned to work and no one questioned me as to where I had been. Everything fell into place and I got my confidence back, as well as my motivation and enthusiasm for work. Upon reflection, perhaps I was a little high at the successful re-integration I had achieved.

The Second Attempt - 1972

There is no valid reason for me to be like this. I have no financial worries and no reason of any kind to be depressed. *The analogies, which I think best fit the situation, are as if I were trying to walk in quicksand, or that someone is pouring treacle on the works.*

It is so difficult to explain: it is the ordinary state of depression, multiplied by a factor of 10,000. For three months, I live in hell. I go to bed at night and hope I will not wake up in the morning. The morning is an extra bad time, as everything crowds in on me. I want to climb back into bed, as this seems the only place of refuge. At these times, I could spend all day in bed. I cannot motivate myself to do anything positive. I have to manage to get myself together somehow, yet the thought of going to work fills me with horror. Meeting people sends a cold chill down my spine.

I have now reached the stage when I feel I cannot continue to work any longer. Work seems to be the main cause of my depression, and I feel I would be much better because of a change. I should add here that throughout this period, I did not visit a doctor as my previous experience with GP's had not been good. Had I access to a consultant psychiatrist, as I do now, the situation would have been far different. With the knowledge I now have, I probably would have been able to resolve my worries.

Now let me return to the story. Having left work, I went away and stayed with some friends, thinking that getting away from everything would give me some respite. I had a glimmer of hope that my health would improve. Then the angry claws of the depression found me again - this time with dire consequences. I decided to take an overdose - I could not put up with those negative feelings any longer. My friends, in what proved to be just just in time, discovered this.

I was rushed to Charing Cross Hospital and was kept in for four days for observation and tests. This time Charing Cross Hospital had a different meaning for me. I wished throughout that stay that I could be anywhere but there, and the predicament I was in. There was nowhere to go and nowhere to hide. I felt that the nurses did not think much of me, although whether this is a true account of things I cannot be sure.

I was then transferred to Springfield Mental Hospital. I will refer here to a couple of points and later will elaborate further. These arise upon reflection, and can be validated now by a more advanced and knowledgeable medical profession, as well as a better-informed patient. There is a myth that a failed suicide attempt is only a call to attract attention, or a cry for help. This can only be put down to ignorance.

In my case, I would say categorically that I did mean to end my life, as I could not see my way out of this profound darkness. The trauma of having failed left me to face up to the reality of coping with life, with the bad feelings I had about myself, and the shame and stigma attached to the act.

Whilst I was being attended by supportive, sympathetic doctors and nurses, there was an occasion, as far as I remember, when attendants pumped out my stomach to rid me of the drugs. This was painful, and I heard the attendants comment: 'let's make it awkward for him, he deserves nothing better.' A consultant psychiatrist, to whom I mentioned this, put it down to ignorance, but emphasised that it should not have been said. He also said it was not my fault that suicide took my will - it was brought on by a state of mind over which I had no control. His reassurances made me feel better, but I continued to feel very down. In hindsight, this would never have happened had I today's facilities and access to hospitals, psychiatrists, counselling and different support organisations.

The Third Attempt - 1975

My condition was deteriorating and my social worker was trying to get me into hospital. I felt that if I was admitted to hospital, I would be better able to deal with the situation. Days were passing and there was no news from the hospital. One evening after work I decided I could take no more. The world was closing in on me - I was in that quicksand again. I did not have any domestic worries as such, yet someone or something was telling me to get out. Perhaps someone can describe it better than me. At this time I discussed it with God. I took two hundred paracetamol tablets; nothing happened except I got very sick.

The next day I was in a quandary and uncertain what to do. I decided to go to the casualty department of my local hospital, the West Middlesex, and I was admitted immediately. My stomach was pumped out and I was told that my kidneys had not been affected. Apparently, if damaged and untreated, the kidneys would wear away over a period of time. I spent a couple of days in a general ward and was then moved to the psychiatric unit. I am convinced that God had saved me once more.

The Fourth Attempt – 1975

This time, lying in hospital, I felt more than ever that I had let others down. A few days passed and I should have gotten out of bed but I refused to get up. I just wanted to lie there - I had not the slightest ambition to move or do anything.

Eventually, the nurses dragged me out of bed. I did not want to eat, but they encouraged me to have some tea and toast. They wanted me to take part in the therapy and games that were going on, but I decided these were options I did not want to take. For days, I remained like this; I just could not interest myself in anything. The nurses excelled in the patience and kindness that they showed towards me: the ward sister in particular tried very hard to get me to play scrabble and other games. I might partake for a little while, but would then have to give up, as I could not sustain concentration. The ward sister would try to engage me in conversation at every opportunity, but I guess it was like taking to a scarecrow, as there was no response from me.

I suppose I had been in hospital for about two weeks, when one morning we were having group therapy, which I had been attending for some days. I did not like the male nurse who was co-coordinating the meeting and had formed that opinion quite early on. It was a dissenting emotion, which added to my negative way of thinking. I can only vaguely recall what happened that day. I felt so bad I became oblivious to my feelings and wanted only to lie down and die.

I recall leaving the hospital buildings, and had not planned to take any particular route. I found myself heading towards the river; part of the journey is hazy, almost as though I was unconscious at times. I arrived at the lock bridge, about one and a half miles from the hospital. I remember standing on it, but not the jump, although I do remember hitting part of the structure as my body descended. The next thing I recall is a police officer in a boat pulling me out of the water. Apparently, it was a bitter cold morning, but I was impervious to the cold - perhaps it was my semi-conscious state.

I cannot recall what happened after my rescue, save being wrapped in a blanket or rug by a kind nurse. I always remember moments of seemingly great kindness to me, and my reaction being one of undeserved-ness. I guess the nurse took me back to the hospital, as the next thing I remember was being in a ward alone with my thoughts. I was moved to the psychiatric unit and lay there feeling battered and bruised with no will to do anything.

My uncle, Mike, came to see me and before he arrived, I was struck by the thought of what could I say to him? Always the height of diplomacy, Uncle Mike did not mention what had happened, in order to spare me embarrassment. It made the first visit easier for me than it might have been, had he been a judgmental man.

I was then told that someone from Unigate was at the hospital, wishing to see me. I became really upset - how could I explain the marks on my face, and the way I looked? Whilst I contemplated this dilemma, the visitor arrived. It was the Assistant Manager with whom I worked. Some of the worry was immediately removed, as I had feared that the visitor would be a member of the Personnel Department. We chatted, and somehow I managed to muster some words of conversation. Nothing was said to embarrass me, nothing was said about the incident and the conversation was mainly about my recovery to health. In all, it was much less of an ordeal than I had anticipated.

The next morning I was up and about. The nurses kept me occupied, and I was feeling much better than I thought I might. That evening, my friends planned to come to see me. Their visit seemed in my mind to be an ordeal to endure. However, everyone seemed to say supportive and kind things to me, and whilst I did not feel that I merited all this fantastic attention, it was having a good effect upon me.

As the days went by, I seemed to improve rapidly, much more so than in previous bouts of illness. The nurses, including the sister, were of tremendous support. If they spotted me moping about, they would get me playing scrabble, arousing in me a better response than before. For some unknown reason, I was feeling much better. One of my friends mentioned that I had said I did not want to see him. I thought he was joking, but another friend referred to a similar remark. This was said to me many months after I had left hospital - I had no recollection of saying this to either of them.

I would not recommend this as a way of being rescued. Again, I had a horrible feeling that this had happened before when I had promised it would never happen again. At these times I hate myself - how can I face the world again? How would I face my Uncle Mike and my friends? It was really good of my Uncle - at no time did he ever bring up the subject. My friends were the same, whether they knew or not. [I mention one friend especially here - Eamonn Coyne. It would be difficult to put into words how good a friend he was, together with his wife Pat.]

5. The Undiagnosed Illness - (Depression)

It was 1967. I was not being monitored by Shenley Hospital or by my GP. I had had one return visit and been declared OK. I had not been told what exactly was wrong with me; as far as I was concerned it was just depression.

I did not know what was wrong with me, only that I was subject to experiencing these terrible depressions. The fact that I had been in mental hospitals suggested that there was something wrong, and I often wrestled with these thoughts. Believe me, that was in itself a trauma. Sometimes I felt I had been hard done by, as I had an extra hurdle to jump over, compared to everyone else. Two priests have said to me independently, having heard about my illness, that it was indeed a heavy cross to carry.

The remarkable thing was that there was no apparent reason for me to be behaving like this. I did not have any worries or problems that would have been the cause of these terrible depressions. Sure, everyone has his or her little problems, and I should be no different in that respect. I underwent a huge loss of confidence during these periods. The word 'happiness' was completely foreign to me. It was as if my whole being was immersed in a quagmire of desolation. My brain seemed stagnant; I could see nothing but doom and gloom. Either at work or socially, I could not see any positive outcomes. Somehow, I just wanted to be left alone. Work constituted the greater part of my day but it was agony to be with colleagues - I felt inhibited and embarrassed in their company. The same applied to my friends; I could not feel enthusiastic about seeing them.

It was as if everyone could see into my mind and read my thoughts. I vividly remember an occasion when I forced myself to go for a walk. On passing a pub, I heard a shout; it was a friend of mine. She

27

invited me in to join her and a few of the circle for a drink - whilst dumbfounded; I could not refuse her request. On joining them, I felt dreadful; I could not contribute to the conversation no matter how hard I tried. Then the humiliation at the comment of, 'Tony, you are exceptionally quiet tonight'. That was one evening I seemed to pass through a hundred hells.

It was 1982, and I was watching myself lest I got a bout of depression after an ordeal I had in Miami, which I will recount later. Doctors and psychiatrists had told me that stress could actuate my mood swings. This depression had made me feel different to every other one. I felt as though I were dirty and inferior to everyone else. It was a lonely feeling, and for everyone's sake I thought I should keep myself to myself. This was the feeling I had from the very first time I entered a mental hospital. In other words, no one would want me and I was by my own admission not worthy of his or her attention or values.

This unknown side of my mental illness was again beginning to surface - this was the exact opposite to the feeling of being depressed. On the contrary, I was feeling confident and good. This abrupt change in mood had happened many times in the past - suddenly having a wonderful feeling of elation. A nurse in a sanatorium once told me I should take care, lest that I might even sell my home without realising it. I did not understand the meaning of her words then, or later.

One thing has often puzzled me throughout my periods of illness - why did the doctors not seem to know, or tell me? Did they think I was naive, a moron, or not sufficiently intelligent to learn or absorb information about my illness? I regard this as a major travesty in my treatment, resulting in a profound effect on my well-being.

Returning to the fear of depression, it was upon my return from America that I was on a roll, really feeling great day and night. I indulged in so many great thoughts, many of my ideas were discarded, and some of them *seemed* valid. I adopted the habit that, whenever I heard or saw an idea or word on the radio or television, straightaway I would write something down to remind me of it. I would write it down on an envelope, a piece of newspaper, or anything that came to hand. Consequently, I wound up with a drawer full of paper. Then, when I went back to research these extracts of wisdom, I had great difficulty, as I never cross-referenced those notes. As I had read somewhere, anything that is to your disadvantage you should turn to your advantage. Thus, the difficulty I had in sorting my notes really helped my memory.

During this period in 1983, my moods were going up and down like a seesaw. What was annoying was that I still did not know anything about the highs, which I could have better enjoyed if I had. They were helping me to make the right decisions, and were smothering my lows. The lows I was experiencing were nothing like, these previous ones - I learned long afterwards that what I was experiencing is known and diagnosed as rapid cycling.

The emphasis, as I thought at the time, was on depression. I must relate that during all this time of investigation, I never once understood what kept me going. There was a hell of a lot going on in my head, and I was coping admirably. I felt so good that anything that was thrown at me, I could contend with. I seemed to have great insight into all my arrangements. It was not until some time later that I discovered that I was a mood swinger.

God must have been on my side through this period. God has deserted me - I always felt that when I prayed for things, they did not happen. In other words, I asked for bonuses and it took a while for me to recognise that I am not always going to get them. Another factor in life is acceptance. I tried very hard with this, and you get what you deserve. I think that the prayer of the alcoholic is just lovely:

'God grant me the serenity to accept the things I cannot change, the courage to change the things that I can, and the wisdom to know the difference'

Nothing else exciting happened in my life, but I was continuing to keep a steady balance. I had gone through some changes that might have upset my stability, yet I seemed to somehow survive all these difficult challenges.

6. Coping with Work

I arrived in England in 1962, saddled with my depression. However, I got a good position with an engineering firm, in the accounts department, and found wonderful accommodation. The depression lifted and life was enjoyable. I had intended to study at night school, but instead worked a lot of overtime. Upon reflection, I regret this, and its relevance in my life will surface later. I remained in this position for four years, then following a disagreement over staffing levels, I moved to a position in Harrow, which, although carried more responsibility, was not well remunerated.

Six months passed, and back came the depression. The work environment did not give rise to a convivial atmosphere - bad practices exacerbated my condition. People were difficult to co-ordinate, e.g. salesmen handing in cheques and foremen supplying information for costing. When my mood was very low, such failures more than irritated me. After just twelve months of being there, I had to quit. Having left, my mood deteriorated further. I found a job that lasted just one day. Irrespective of job opportunities, I could not handle the post once in place.

In the doldrums, and almost wiped out on the floor, I had also known for some time that my parents were ill: my mother had angina and my father was suffering from a terminal cancer. Whether these factors had any bearing on what was to come remains to be seen. I struggled in my dreadful state to apply for a vacancy in Victoria. To my huge surprise, I received a reply and attended an interview held by an imposing company team, a member of the personnel department, the assistant secretary and the Company Secretary. They offered me the position, and this in another state would have thrilled me. However, there was a cloud of depression around me, and in me. It is difficult to explain how it is to feel lethargic, but doubly so. I

31

worked for two weeks in my new job, and then came back to that downhill feeling, only this time multiplied by a factor of ten.

I had managed to stay off the beer for some time - six months to be precise. At the end of the six months, I was sitting in a bar in Victoria with my colleagues. I had my glass of ginger ale. We were celebrating someone's birthday. The firm employed up to 2000 office staff including draughtsmen, engineers, architects, accounts staff etc. Even though one did not belong to the department from where the birthday person came, we enjoyed the privilege of extra time in the bar. I was fed up drinking ginger ale and turned to brandy, and so this turned into a real session.

It was a Bank Holiday weekend and there was much work to be done - there was a large payroll to be made ready. We finally dragged ourselves away from the pub and returned to the office. We had to work overtime to complete the job on time. A few others and myself continued to nip out to the pub during the course of the evening (not the done thing!). Some of us offered to come in on Saturday when we would be in a better condition, but to no avail. I had arranged to go dancing with some friends that evening, in a venue in Victoria. When I got to the pub, some of my friends could not contain their mirth. I was in such a state of inebriation; I was 'king of the castle'. I had words with the barman....

Eventually, my friends managed to persuade me to leave with them for the dance, so off we all went.... I was told off by a couple of girls for my behaviour - luckily I knew them. The next day, I regretted what had happened and felt bad throughout the weekend. I was detailed to go to Shenley for a post-check up on the Tuesday that followed. This was bothering me - its outcome and how I would deal with it.

I had the interview at Shenley and all went well. The doctors were pleased with my progress. I was apprehensive, as I was disappointed with myself due to the happenings of the weekend. When I returned to London, and to work, I had to attend an interview with the Assistant Secretary about the episode prior to the Bank Holiday. I received a dressing down for neglecting the urgency of my work, and I agreed that my behaviour had been out of order. At another time this would have had a bad effect upon me and would have certainly brought on depression. On this occasion, I seemed able to cope and maintained my confidence. It did not mean that I took the incident lightly.

I had now been a year with Humphreys and Glasgow, having joined them in 1967. Life was great, as I never would have imagined. I had become part of a group of friends, about twenty in all, and I was active socially.

My employment at Humphreys and Glasgow was now entering its sixth year, 1973. Loss of contracts had reduced the workload and the opportunity for overtime. Our salaries took a dive, as this extra earning cushion was taken away. I was lucky - I was offered a part-time job with Esso Petroleum working on analysis and statistics, so when I finished my daytime job I walked out the door and into my evening job.

The fallacy of working overtime is that it gives one a false sense of personal economic status and standard of living. Then one has to climb down when it is taken away as, financially, one is worse off. It did not enter my head that I could have taken time to set myself up to do some learning and have a better-balanced life socially. I could have done with a rest, to get things into perspective; I guess it was difficult for me to consider what a normal life was after all the years of work, work, and work. My focus was on the additional money I earned and, to a certain extent, working long hours was a consolation - this life-style seemed therapeutic. After all, it seemed that the greater part of the social life I had had was visiting the pub or playing badminton or tennis - not so much to miss.

Life seemed good. I carried on with my work, and felt quite competent in my ability to do the job. The company's workload was being reduced and, consequently, some of the staff left. A number of my colleagues (and friends) were affected, and I was sad to see them go. On the other hand, this might mean promotion for me. My social life was fine; all was well in work and play. Then, after about two months, I felt all my confidence draining away, leaving me with the feeling that there was no way out.

One of my friends ran a staff agency, and was able to offer me a position as a temporary accounts clerk. This was an unforeseen opportunity to help me to cope with the changes taking place. I discovered that, if one could adapt to taking one day at a time, it would be of immense value. In truth, I have only taken this genuinely on board of late. Things may be different tomorrow, but it is better not to predict.

Working as a temp meant I could avoid awkward questions from prospective employers, as to mention a subject such as mental health would have destined me for the door. Sadly, people like me have to live out our lives under such clouds. We have to be careful that our mental condition is not discovered without our admission, and it should not be written or mentioned as a causal factor at any time. I did not wish to lie, or to keep it a secret, but saying nothing seemed the safest option.

Would I have to carry this cross along with the others throughout my life?

My temporary post was with the London Borough of Hammersmith. I do not know how I survived the first day, and was certainly not looking forward to the next. I continued to feel very depressed. The work was not demanding, and I could work at my own pace. As I went to work each day I envied other people, and thought how happy they seemed with their work and with the world in general. It was a pleasant environment, and the people were nice. There was no pressure upon me, and yet I could not shake off my misery - felt it all a strain. At the time, I did not see how it was enabling me to re-integrate into society. The remuneration was low, but this seemed unimportant at the time.

At work, the clerical union raised objection to my being employed on a part-time basis, so full-time employment was the prospect if I were to remain there. I suffered no animosity on this point; the staff were affable in their insistence, and just as well, as this could have had a deeply upsetting affect upon me.

I remained there for about four months. The work was monotonous, and so I began to look for another position. This signified some small show of ambition - a welcome change of state. I had noticed a position with a company called Firestone, which I applied for and was called for an interview. This was a boost to my morale. I was successful in obtaining the post - I must have looked better on the outside than I felt on the inside. The job was promising; the office was pleasant, my own payroll to manage, a very nice general manager and staff. Another bonus was that I could drive to work and this was pleasing as driving gave me confidence. Was this all too good to be true?

The one fly in the ointment was in the form of the assistant manager - an unpleasant type who decided to pick on me. To put up with his constant jibes would have been counterproductive and I knew I would have to leave, in spite of all the advantages I had initially perceived. Some three months after I had joined Firestone, I left. I felt this was the right thing to do, because to stay would have caused a daily hassle. This would have got me down, and, crucially, I was improving slowly, day by day.

Whilst not noticeable at the time, I was at least making decisions about an important element in my life. For a depressed person, any decision is a major feat - putting it off until the last minute means a decision can hardly be made. I was able to arrange temporary employment through my friends' staff agency prior to handing in my notice at Firestones - a welcome safety net. Gradually, I was emerging from those dark corridors of despair. I could sense a change in my being, and felt some purpose to my life.

My next job was with a firm called Rambutan. They had subsidiary companies, which ran clubs, pubs and restaurants throughout England. The position involved bookkeeping and payroll responsibilities. It was difficult to begin with, as none of the managers had any knowledge of book keeping procedures. The company was open to my advice, and gave me a free hand to improve recording procedures. My manager was an easygoing person and I got along with him. The most difficult day's work occurred on Mondays, when time sheets and returns arrived. The bulk of the accounts came in with the managers themselves and the balance by post. Those that came by post were sorted out over the telephone, with some trepidation on my part.

Payroll was a difficult area in which to educate the managers. As their business was leisure, they had all categories of workers from part-time, full-time, self-employed to temporary; men, women, boys and girls - all on different pay scales and all with different National Insurance categories. To the managers, one national insurance card looked just the same as the next.

A major compensation in the midst of the unintended confusion and annoyance was the debonair extrovert personalities of the managers, clad in their bright clothes. They were amiable to deal with, and once methods were explained, they did try to comply with good practice. The nature of the work, and the style of the managers, was gradually lifting me from my depression - it was a slow process but I was getting somewhere at last.

Pub managers were sometimes so careless in their recording that an on-site audit became necessary, and these were always enjoyable to me. A few months ago, such a task would have been inconceivable. At last, there seemed to be light at the end of the tunnel. Maybe not a spring in my step, but the dragging footsteps seemed to be disappearing. Should there be something good to come out of such a long period of despair, it was the special feeling of getting well and back to some semblance of normality.

Rambutan owned a chain of restaurants, known as Flanagan's, and our office was located over one of these in Kensington. I was allowed to eat in the restaurant every day, being served by tall elegant girls. This was much better than the meals and atmosphere of Springfield Hospital. Working in fashionable Kensington helped to elevate my mood, and lent me new perspectives.

Opposite the offices was the Royal Garden Hotel, where the rich and famous passed through the doors every day. At lunchtime, I could walk down the High Street, visiting the high-class department stores that then adorned this thoroughfare. At that time, Biba was just establishing itself. Its followers, and my mingling with that crowd, were having an effect upon me. When I contrast these experiences to a time when I was depressed - given the same situation, I would have been oblivious to all that was around me.

Confident in my professional abilities, I applied for a position at Unigate, but, when I spoke to their personnel department, I was advised I was not qualified to do the job. At another time, that would have been a huge blow to my ego, but on good form, I could take it in my stride.

I had registered with a couple of employment agencies, and the next day one of them telephoned me to say he had arranged for me to attend an interview with Unigate. I told him I had already been in contact with their personnel department, and of their advice. My agency contact felt I should go to the interview: I had nothing to lose except a little time. A few days later, I went to Unigate and met the manager and deputy of the payroll department.

Everything went fine - they both questioned me on specific aspects of payroll and costing. They gave me some sheets of payroll to balance and evaluate, and I seemed to pass the test. They then asked if I had any experience of a system of payroll as operated under the National Cash Register procedure. I replied that that system had been one I had worked with at Humphreys and Glasgow for five years. To this, the manager replied: "I once visited Humphreys and Glasgow to learn about their operating system." This provided us with a topic of mutual interest, and the pros and cons of converting to new payroll systems. Unigate was currently employing the NCR system and were looking to other options. My interview ended, and the manager and assistant excused themselves from my presence for a few minutes. Upon their return, they announced that the position was mine.

My depression was really lifting now, allowing my confidence to return. It had been a long haul returning to what I could call good health. Here, we can see that the experience of depression lifting is no easier to explain than its arrival. Generally, when people feel low it can be attributed to emotional disturbances such as bereavement, post-natal depression or the result of serious physical illness or injury. My case was different, as I discovered much later, but for many years I remained utterly uneducated in the nature of my condition. It was different from all diagnosed forms of depression. When I discovered exactly what my illness was, I wanted to explain what I have learned about it and my experiences of it. However, it is as difficult for me to explain the cause and effect, as it is for others to understand.

In the meantime, I began my employment at Unigate. The payroll department comprised four people, each with their own responsibilities. My three colleagues were very helpful and enabled me to settle in easily. I was enjoying my social life and felt like a new person. I was happy to have a drink with my friends, enjoyed their company again, as well as the beer, and having a few drinks did not seem to be a vision of looming alcoholism.

I was playing tennis again, and took an interest in the company football team - all of these interests were stimulating. At work, a ritual on a Friday afternoon was a session at a local pub - this could only take place after the balancing of books had been achieved. Not wishing to appear unsocial, wanting to be part of the group, I went along with them. This may seem like an excuse on my part, but truthfully, I was trying to avoid alcohol as much as I could. In the event, the outcomes of the Friday sessions were a few drinks, and everyone getting to know one another better.

I owe a great debt to this particular group of colleagues, as they helped me so much in my recovery, and procured a raise in salary for me after a preliminary six-month period had been successfully completed. As I preferred to start work early, they had my hours of work re-structured to take this into account. They arranged for me to work overtime when it was needed, and this was well remunerated. They introduced me to the Social Club, which was located on the plant, and enabled me to become a member - a certain privilege, as it was intended for plant, rather than office, personnel.

The social club held many outings and events, and was a great social outlet for me. Travel opportunities to

Europe and games of golf, were two of the many things I enjoyed through their facilities. I visited many golf courses in the south east of England, enjoying playing until my back began to be troublesome. I wasn't a great player, but I enjoyed the atmosphere and being outdoors. I also went fishing and to the races. It was also at this time that high blood pressure began to bother me. I had some minor blackouts, and was given medication and advised to take things easy.

1974

A few months passed and I could feel the pangs of depression arriving again. This was a real disappointment for me, as it was such a short time since I had last experienced them. I was given a social worker based in Chiswick, who I could see on the way home from work. This was a good arrangement, as it saved my having to take time off. No suspicions were aroused, there were no risks of anyone finding out about my illness, no threats of being marginalised - all of which are fears that haunt me, whether I am sick or well.

I made arrangements to return to work. For some reason, I felt confident in taking this step. In another time, and in another mood, I would not have been looking forward to this - I would have been embarrassed and ashamed of myself, of all that had happened. I returned to work and slotted into place, seemingly taking things in my stride. In some respects, it seemed as though nothing had happened and there was no need for embarrassment on my part. My colleagues had assured the company that they would cover the workload in my absence. Such nobility and loyalty on their part touched me deeply, and gave me the confidence I required. Weeks passed and I was back to an equable state, feeling part of the team at work and enjoying my social life with my friends.

The first part of 1976 was a good time for me; work was fine, I was doing a lot of overtime, and availing myself of the outings and activities organised by the Social Club. I could say life was normal, with no signs of depression, and my thoughts positive and rational. I was meeting people, going out with my friends and confident in all I was doing.

In the summer of 1976, I became involved with the Trade Union movement through my work. I studied the philosophy of the movement, its structure and form of association. Its principles were to be admired, but they were not always adhered to, a discovery I later made.

On joining Unigate, I had become a member of the Union of Clerical Workers, which was optional at that time.

After a year had passed, I had become more active in the Union Branch, wanting to be involved in issues of staff welfare, etc. It was not a question of 'them and us'. I wanted a good dialogue with the company, good working conditions for the staff, and for the company to thrive and prosper. All of these were sincere thoughts and ambitions - perhaps I was a little green. I will return to this involvement with the Union later.

I began my Union Studies on a day release system at Slough College of Technology. I was attending study seminars, sometimes for a week at a time, and the learning experience was proving to be beneficial for me mentally. Getting about and meeting people, and finding out about things. I found out to my astonishment that I was capable of writing an essay, and this achievement was very important to my self-esteem.

1979

The workload at Unigate had fallen off. Overtime was no longer available and so I took on a part-time weekend job, carrying out stock taking audits in supermarkets and large shops. Life was full, my mental faculties were well occupied, and remuneration for all my efforts was fine.

1980

This was a good year up to the autumn, and what transpired then was an indication and influence of how things were to be in the following years. At the time, it seemed coincidence was at play - later it became clear that this was not the case. At work, changes were taking place, and computerisation was being extended to all departments. People were concerned about job security - would their future be at risk because of the technical expansion programme?

Being a Union representative, I was involved in the negotiations between staff and management. Unigate was planning to computerise a vast geographical area, including ours, the London region. The implications were that the entire accounting operation would be housed under one umbrella based at the Trowbridge office, resulting in the loss of many jobs and the lowering of employee status.

The Union felt that that part of the organisation, which had already been computerised, was not at all efficient. The negotiations were to go on for a long period, and the Union finally conceded that partial expansion could go ahead. The negotiations were vigorously contested, and staff received substantial bonuses for the loss of privileges. The talks between management and union were to continue for some time and I realised that I had placed myself under a twofold trigger of pressure. I ran for election as chair of the union branch and was elected. I wanted to become chairman for several reasons, the primary one was the power to control a meeting, as I felt that this would give me the confidence I lacked - to be in front of people and have to speak in public was frightening for me.

Negotiations were continuing at Unigate and I would be influential acting in a different role as the branch union chair. It may have been a poor exchange for what would be the inevitable loss of jobs, but good bonus payments were being made in offers of redundancy compensation.

For some time, I had been disillusioned with the running of the Union, and the hierarchical nature of its structure. I discovered that one of the paid officials, a district officer, had canvassed against my election to the chair, and now that same official was interfering in branch affairs. There were other issues that disappointed me; whilst I remained in agreement with all of the principles of the Union, the carrying out of these in a democratic manner left a lot to be desired.

I decided to sever my association with the Union of Clerical Workers, as I was disgusted by the manipulations of those in authority. Their care and concern was neither for their members, nor for the Union's principles. They abused their elected positions to further their own power seeking. Ironically, the voting power of the members had the capacity to change the leadership, but they did not use it for this purpose. A group of twenty of us tried to set up an alternative Union, but we had to abandon our attempts due to lack of support and resources.

All throughout this period, my studies at the Open University enabled me to achieve a great deal of learning experience, which could contribute in turn to my future studies.

1981

At work, the scene was changing rapidly. Our manager had been transferred, and aspects of the payroll operation were being moved. Cosy arrangements were being disrupted by all of this: computerisation was being introduced, staff underwent training and anxieties were felt about the eventual outcome for job tenure.

I often now wonder how I managed to hold down a full-time job at Unigate, do a part-time job at the weekend, and study for a degree at the Open University, all at the same time. Nobody noticed anything peculiar about me throughout this time, and I most certainly did not question the deployment of my time. I recall feeling good, feeling confident without knowing why, being on the high side. It was just a month later that I felt a depression coming on, my confidence, true or false, disappearing fast.

I contacted the psychiatric unit I was attending and saw them almost immediately. Having a chat with someone and being able to talk through my situation was a great help. I was attending my three monthly meetings at the unit, managing to fulfil all my obligations. At this point, I quit my part-time weekend job as it was becoming too demanding, and took on a security post part-time instead.

There was a rumour circulating around Unigate that closure of the firm was imminent. This gossip and uncertainty added to the frustration of not knowing the results of my first examination at the Open University. It was in March that Unigate advised its workforce that it was closing and that all were to be made redundant. This was more or less what we all had been expecting as the rumours had been flying around for some time. It demoralised me and I felt my luck was batting zero. If it rained soup, I would be bound to have a fork in my hand!

May was the redundancy month for the office staff, and for the factory staff it followed a few months later.

At the end of May 1983 I was made redundant at Unigate, something that some years later was regarded as a major trauma in anyone's life. Prior to my notice, I had looked for another job, applying for numerous positions and even attended some interviews. I was 47 years of age, and this was a deciding factor in my future. This was the beginning of the downsizing of companies.

I found temporary accounting work through an employment agency, and one assignment I will expand on was one at Penguin Books. The chief accountant had given me a brief outline as to the work he wanted me to undertake. I was covering a long-term absence through sickness in the wages section, a managerial post. There was a pension return to be finalised initially, as it had fallen into arrears over several months. The chief accountant told me that there would be a director based at the office a few times a month, and that he would help me. Should there be anything else I needed to know, the director held the information on the pension tabulation. It turned out that he was not prepared to share this information, for whatever reasons he wished to keep it to him self.

Additionally, I had to contend with four women working on the payroll, and any questions I asked, yielded no informative responses. I suspect that they thought I was destined to be the new payroll manager, and some of them harboured ambitions for themselves in that post. As for the director himself, he came into the office for a few hours every other day. Any attempt to extract information from him met with similar reactions, and as for the pension return, I dug and dug to extrapolate the merest piece of helpful knowledge. The chief accountant was a nice person, and I felt bad when after three weeks of being there I decided to quit. The director, when I told him, said: 'what will I tell Mr. so and so?' My response was that it was his problem to solve.

I fulfilled a few more assignments for the agency, and then decided I had had enough. The only alternative I could think was to become a full time security officer...not much of a job, but there was little choice on the horizon. As I had already done this work part time, I at least knew what to expect. I would also be able to carry on studying without neglecting my security duties.

At first, I worked short time - two weekend shifts at one site and three shifts during the week. After a month had passed, I moved to a new site - The Royal Festival Hall. Here I was working five six-hour shifts, 5pm to 11pm, and being paid double time. It had its plus and minus points: I got to meet a very pleasant clientele on the plus side and kept up-to-date with concerts and exhibitions. On the downside, there were the vagrants that strayed into the foyer, being on your feet for the entire time of the shift, and relieving the place of ticket touts.

I was then relocated to a firm making printing presses, and my hours were twelve-hour night shifts starting at 4.30pm. I struck a good deal in remuneration with my employers as the hours were so unsociable - they were a good firm to be contracted to. Nice people, and appreciative of my thoroughness. In between doing my security checks on the building and adjoining yard, I was able to carry out my studies. From 5pm-7pm I covered reception - the staff finished at 5pm, but the managers and directors stayed on until around 7pm. I was on good terms with the directors, and on occasion would have a chat with them. I was particularly friendly with the managing director. He knew that I was studying and would always show an interest in my progress.

It was 1983 and the early part of the year passed. I was relatively happy, making the best of work. The directors of the company that I was contracted to were very kind to me. I used to remark to myself that when the office staff finished their day's work, or when they were in contact with me, they had a patronising attitude that I was just the security man. In my younger days, we called that attitude, 'tuppence looking down on three ha'pence'. It was such a contrast to the attitude of the directors!

Ever since I had left Unigate, I had been wishing to find a job in accounts or personnel, but nothing seemed to be available to me. My age worked against me, although I was unaware of this at the time.

Over the next few weeks I felt elated, (yet another of those highs had overtaken me), and I recall a sort of arrogance on my part. I remember one of the managers coming to see me; I knew this was out of concern, and we chatted for a long time. He must have been satisfied that I was OK.

Socially, I was uptight and restless. Overall, I felt I ought to visit my GP. He was not there, but a locum was, and he gave me a medical certificate, which I did not read until I got home. When I did read it, I felt a huge sense of annoyance - hyper mania was the stated condition on the medical certificate that I was to show to my employers. The following day I went to the psychiatric unit wanting to see a doctor. The receptionist said that I would need an appointment, and this technicality annoyed me even further.

I informed her that I had been attending the psychiatric unit for a long time - long before her appointment - and that the doctors had told me I could come at any time. She went off to see someone and a few minutes later, the doctor whom I had been seeing appeared. She took me into her office and commented that I had been rude to the receptionist.

I said that I had been upset with the description the doctor had put on the medical certificate issued, and because of this, I could not give it to my employer. She read it for herself and agreed with the predicament in which it placed me. She issued another certificate, which used the words 'nervous exhaustion'. I was satisfied, and went and bought the receptionist some flowers, telling her I had not meant to be offensive. I also bought the doctor a bottle of wine. I was a few bob out of pocket, but what the hell - I felt no remorse about my reaction or behaviour.

Having had a few days off, my mood changed, and I felt reluctant to return to the monotony of my job. I had had the thought of running a pub for some years - it was not a spur of the moment thought. Whilst I had discussed it once with a doctor at the psychiatric unit, I felt it was time to discuss it again.

I went to see my doctor and he advised against it - he felt it could be a stressful enterprise and not suitable for me. However, I could not get it out of my system, and thought that perhaps the best way to test it would be to find a job in a bar and get some work experience. I did this for three months, but I found the hours very long, my studies were being neglected, and furthermore, I really did not like the work. I started at 8.30am and finished at midnight, with a break in between of two and a half hours. A decision had to be made and, even if it meant unemployment, I would try to find other work, which would be more satisfying and allow the time I needed for my studies.

I had been looking for a suitable permanent job in what was one of the worst eras in contemporary times for unemployment levels. Whilst despondent, I was not depressed and was able to credit myself as having survival power. It was July and there were no prospects of employment. I had applied for so many posts without luck. It was soul-destroying, but I tried to bolster my spirits with my Open University studies. These were a tremendous help and therapy, and kept me mentally and physically occupied. I had been attending Schizophrenic Fellowship meetings and these were also a great support

At last I found a job through the labour exchange. I had seen advertisements for postal vacancies in central London and decided to apply. I was interviewed, tested and accepted, and the remuneration was not too low. I marked out a work pattern: providing it was acceptable to my supervisor, I would work afternoon shifts inside, sorting post and so on, rather than outside work, i.e. delivering letters and parcels.

The mandatory policy was that one had to alternate between the two on a six-monthly cycle. Whilst working inside, I had to undergo some tests to check my familiarity with the streets, towns, and counties that came within the sorting frames. For the first six months of the sorting work, I had to be out of bed at 4.30am to be at work at 6am. Outside work saw me commencing at 1.30pm and finishing at 10pm. In this large Central London sorting office, there were approximately three thousand employees of all classes, races and creeds; the turnover in personnel was over 60% per week.

I mention all this to make a particular point. In the locker rooms, where there were about five hundred workers sharing at any given time, the level of hygiene is poor. Even on the work floor, I sorted alongside colleagues whose personal hygiene was atrocious. When people intend to stay a week at a job, they do not seem to care what they do. There were instances of people using drugs, and I was not given any help or information. It was pitiful to see women acting in a macho way, trying to compete with the bullishness of the men - they lost any small part of the femininity they possessed.

The supervisors and managers were promoted from the shop floor without any leadership or management training, or people skills. Being subordinate to them was like being a foot soldier in the worst type of army. The environment of the post office, in those days, was devoid of intelligence either on the shop floor, or in the management.

I had applied for a clerical post in administration, which had been advertised internally. A month later I had not received a response. I saw the Postmaster and discussed this with him and he promised me that he would look into it. A few days later I received a reply - I was unsuitable. As far as I can recall, no further reason was given.

Some time later, I made discreet inquiries to an inspector as to how such decisions were reached. He informed me that, in my case, my previous involvement with the Trade Union movement was the reason for their decline. I continued with my work, feeling somewhat depressed at this news, but was determined to not let it get me down. Perhaps this episode seems very biased in my favour, but the Post Office was not a suitable working environment for me - in my state of health I needed it like a hole in the head!

I was soon be working the afternoon shift, which affected my social life and my tutorials with the Open University. Some inspectors were reasonable and allowed me to take time off to attend tutorials when necessary, but often I had to work time in lieu. The following few months were dreary and, working late shifts, once I had arrived at the building it was Goodbye Mr. Chips.

All around the West End theatres, people were going out and enjoying their evenings. I felt sorry for the fathers working on the late shift - they rarely got to see their children, or have any form of social or home life. At least I was saving some money, as otherwise I would have been socialising or going to the pub. Christmas was approaching - a very busy time for the Royal Mail. I started to do delivery rounds and decided that these were definitely not my cup of tea. I had been working inside for some weeks, and now that I had to work outside, the weather was cold, it was snowing and I had to get up at 4.30am, even on Christmas Eve. I trudged the streets around Holborn in the cold feeling miserable.

I struggled away at work whilst longing to be doing something else. I passed a number of sorting tests and my training finished. I was now a fully qualified postman. I was doing afternoon shifts and, after a few months passed, I was given the job of sorting franked post. This meant that I was working on my own, which at least it kept me away from the others. Whilst monotonous, I at least achieved some sort of peace of mind. Because of this working pattern, my life was devoid of social time and I could only go out at weekends. I was drinking very little, and was beginning to see clearly the correlation between my drinking and mood swings.

I was given the opportunity to change my job but, after consideration, decided to stay put with the one I had. Whilst it was boring, there was no interference from anyone. The bouts of depression came and went, but I was able to handle them better.

Early in the New Year of 1988, I changed my job at the Post Office to a position where I continued to work alone. This new job, though tedious and dusty, was compensated for by a friendly supervisor. He allowed me to make alternative work arrangements to enable me to attend the tutorials required as part of my study work. The job consisted of sorting bags of mail, and dispatching mail to and from the post office railway, which runs underneath London. I also had to arrange frames for sorting purposes. The atmosphere was agreeable and my mood stable.

Then yet another blow was to strike me - I contracted arthritis. At the end of May I received a letter from the hospital, telling me that my appointment with the consultant would take place during the first week in July. A week later, I received a letter from the Post Office requesting details of my illness from the hospital. Forgetting that they had already received confirmation of my problems from my doctor, I asked the hospital to write. They wrote a letter, which gave a record of my medication, including the prescription for Lithium. I requested that it be rewritten, as I did not wish my employers to know that I was a mood swinger. Woe would be me if they were to discover this.

I struggled on until July when I was to see the consultant. I went to the hospital with feelings of apprehension and, when I arrived, I was surprised to find I would see his understudy. I was thoroughly examined by her, and she quickly diagnosed that I had rheumatoid arthritis. She sent me for an x-ray, prescribed drugs and gave me a list of exercises to carry out. She told me to get bags of frozen peas and to put them on my hands to relieve the swelling. This may seem comical, but it works. It took two weeks for the swelling to go down and people thought that once this had been achieved, the pain would disappear. The sad thing was that it remained.

I would sit in front of the television with splints on my hands to try to alleviate the pain. During the course of the day, my legs would swell up and this would not subside until I rested at night. My back and hips were almost constantly painful and the medication I was taking gave but temporary relief. It did not help my mental state, as arthritis has a tendency to cause depression. I do not know how I resisted going down.

A letter arrived from the Post Office to say that I was to have an interview with their doctor. Whilst travelling on public transport is very uncomfortable due to my condition, I went along and had a long and thorough examination. He advised me that I would be informed by post as to the result of this ordeal. I returned home and wondered whether I would be dismissed. If that were to happen, what would I do? It had been difficult to get the job at the Post Office in the first place. What would be my chances of getting a position anywhere else? How was I going to live and manage financially?

Because of changing jobs and the lack of continuity of employment, I had not been able to transfer any of my superannuation. My pension entitlement, therefore, would be meagre. I had no idea what my state pension entitlement would be and I was terribly disturbed by all of these worries. It nearly drove me around the bend, although most people thought I had already gone around it!

A few weeks elapsed and the news arrived from the Post Office that I had been dismissed. I became more positive and thought that I was better off out of it, having detested the place whilst I was there. Something would turn up. A few weeks later my finances looked a bit better, and I had a Social Security communiqué concerning my entitlements to disability pension and so on. These were welcome, and gave me a sense of relief.

7. Education

I had studied correspondence courses with the Union of Clerical Workers, to which I belonged, and officiated for, during the course of my employment at Unigate. At the time of these early studies, I saw an advertisement for the Open University. It stated that Trade Union representation was one of a number of qualifying factors for enrolment. I decided to apply.

When I received the acceptance letter, I was overcome with joy - it was as though they had already awarded me a degree. Before embarking on the scheme, I took a preparatory course in Technology to equip me for the main study programme. I will always remember my first tutorial, and my comment to the tutor of: 'I am not good enough for this'. His reply was: 'you are here, are you not?' For every course I passed following that first one, I repeated his comment to myself. This preparatory course was to continue until Christmas 1981. I found it difficult at first, as studying was new territory for me.

In January 1982, I registered for my first Open University courses - Technology and Social Science. This was ridiculously over-ambitious, but I did know I was on a high. The thinking that led me to this decision was that I was getting older, and if I could achieve two courses, rather than one, per year, I would get my degree in three years. Wishful thinking on my part, because even a well qualified student would not have attempted to study two courses simultaneously. My mood swings were running away with my ambition, and as it was, I was feeling inhibited at doing the first part of my preparatory course.

I commenced my main studies in February and things initially went well. Just over a month had passed since my studies commenced, and I had received good results in both of my first assignments for each of the courses I was following.

My counsellor at the Open University advised me to withdraw from one of the courses, so I cancelled Technology and continued with Social Science. My tutor at the Open University gave me special help and attention as education-wise; all of the other students were streets ahead of me. I was however, catching up fast, and one tutor gave me the advice to ask questions when subjects were discussed of which I had little or no knowledge.

Working as a part-time security guard in 1982 enabled me to extend my reading time - the work it self was not demanding mentally. I was due to attend a summer school at Bath University, and I was not looking forward to this at all. Being in an unfamiliar formal environment, and having to meet new people, scared the hell out of me. It would be fair to say that many of the students planning to attend the summer school were going through the same qualms as I, but as I was on a downer, it all seemed to be more than I could face.

Somehow, I battled through the depression and when the end of August came, I knew that I had to attend the school in order to be successful with my studies. I arrived on campus in a petrified state. Not only was I depressed, but also felt somewhat overwhelmed surrounded by what I perceived as budding academics. I regarded myself as something of a tramp scholar. Perhaps this was a good attitude for me to adopt - it meant I could only go up in the world.

The first meeting of the students and tutors went okay, and when the tutor said that we should introduce ourselves to the person sitting next to us, I was lock-jawed with embarrassment. The lady alongside suffered no such inhibitions and had enough to say for both of us. I am being cruel here - she was very pleasant and we did have a good conversation.

After a few days of attending lectures and speaking to other students, I began to settle in. I was still feeling very low and knew nothing about it would be easy, but I had to make a good go of things for the sake of my studies. I attended classes and lectures from 9am to 9pm, punctuated by a few short breaks in between. I met up with students socially, and met a girl who suffered from anorexia nervosa. This was the first time I had met someone with this condition and, in the mornings as we bumped into each on our way to tutorials, she would leave me at the cafeteria saying she must have a quick bite of breakfast. Other students then told me that she passed straight through the cafeteria. Most of my group seemed to know her and her habits well. This made me question if they knew that they had another 'left-hander' in their midst - myself.

By the end of the week, I could feel the depression lifting. This was a huge relief and a new way of living was beginning to take place in me. There was no promise of an instant cure, but a slow steady road to stability. The Open University was as the home I had always longed for - not only was it educating me, it was grooming me into a better person. I had faults for sure, but before they had made me feel dirty and guilty, and they never seemed to go away.

You can see from my story so far that, largely, I felt my life had been a mess. Because of the Open University I could now perceive myself more truly. I can pay it no higher tribute than to say it became my cerebral home. Home is where the heart is. Following on from that, the heart is charity and charity is love. Love is what makes the world go round. For me, such a small four-letter word contains all the good things in life. Unfortunately, I have suffered rejection because of my mood swings so it is not surprising that I found love in the Open University. That first summer school made me feel a lot more confident and better informed in relation to my studies, and to my fellow students.

Throughout the summer months of 1982, my slow improvement continued. By the time my examination arrived in October, I was in a fairly good, and prepared, state of mind. Of course I was terribly nervous, as I had not sat an examination in many years. Somehow, I got through the exam paper, and hoped I would have a good chance of passing. Then came the long wait until December for the results. I had been coping well with all my duties up to that time. The fact that I had dealt with my depression, and avoided repeating any of the errors of the past, made me feel as though at last I could put a feather in my cap.

The week before Christmas, I received the long awaited results of my examination - to my great joy I had passed. It took me four hours to open that envelope and it was the most wonderful Christmas present I ever received. I recalled those words of response from my tutor in the summer - 'you are here'. One of my other tutors commented that I would derive more satisfaction from passing that exam than other students, whose formal educational achievements were far greater than mine were.

Early in January 1983, I registered with the Open University for the Technology course from which I had withdrawn the previous year. It was a formidable challenge and, whilst I had a varied interest in the subject throughout my adult life, I knew hardly anything about it. I knew a little about a lot, and not enough about any one thing. This attitude was my approach to all the Open University courses I took; I was too light for heavy work and too heavy for light work. I did not recognise it at the time, but I must have relished challenge. Perhaps I was trying to make up for my lack of inches. Being of small stature, the joke that I shared with my friends was that God made me that way; if I had been made tall, the human race could not have withstood me.

The first few months of study progressed satisfactorily, even though the subject was relatively new, and was now was being presented in a sophisticated fashion through the Open University. I could see academic types in the Technology students around me, and I saw that a rapport would not arise. For them, Technology came out of a textbook, whereas I was old fashioned, and knew it had been around for quite some time. I always had the belief that no matter what we had in life, it was an extension of what had already been there before. If I could combine the knowledge in the textbooks with the expertise that had always been there - and a little good luck - I might obtain a first on the course...

It was now October and I sat my Technology examination, followed again by that wait until Christmas for the result. Again, I could not open the envelope, but no matter how long I resisted, the information would be the same, so I eventually did find out. When I finally opened it, I was bitterly disappointed - I had failed. This was such a downer for me - it had been a lousy year, and I could only feel that I had been kicked up the pants at the end of it. I could re-sit the examination, but that would not be until the following October.

Early in the New Year of 1984, I saw the doctor in the psychiatric unit of my local hospital; I told him I was thinking of querying my examination result with the Open University. We chatted about it, and he said that even though I failed by a mere two marks, an appeal now would cause a lot of hassle for little return. We decided instead, as far as I can remember, that I would study for the re-sit later in the year, and that I should not take on another course, as it would be too much for me. I felt very reassured by this talk, and got on well with this doctor. I regretted that I would see him again just once before he moved on, as he was a trainee, and due to be moved on.

October came, along with the time for my examination re-takes. Exam time is stressful for most people, and much more so for me on this occasion, because I simply had to pass. There would not be another opportunity, no second re-take, so with my fingers firmly crossed I entered the examination room. At the end of the examination, I felt I had done as much as I could to pass this time.

Nothing much happened in the dreaded wait until Christmas, except my well-being continued mentally. Christmas week arrived, as did the envelope containing the exam result. Half the day passed and I still could not open it. I was all nerves, trying to read the letter through the envelope. Upon opening it, I found I was reading the letter upside down. Finally, I turned it the right way up and the result was positive - I had passed. It was a huge boost, and again I thought of those words the tutor uttered when I started out at the Open University. I enrolled on an Economics course for the following year, 1985.

I had ambitions that I might become an Information Technologist if I could get my degree. I wrote to Information Scientists and, in their reply, they stated that I would need librarian qualifications as well as my degree.

I was lucky enough to obtain an interview with the Head of Education in Hounslow. He and I enjoyed a good discussion, and he gave me details of where to find relevant courses in librarianship. I was very grateful to him and it was so easy to speak to him that I left not knowing whether I was embarrassed or proud of the time he gave me.

I researched the opportunities and there was no way I could fit in another course at this time. I was cynical within, and at times like this I would say to myself, 'perhaps when I am sixty-five!'

In February, I commenced my Open University course in Economics and received a good result for my first assignment. My tutor was very good to me during those early days of study and of tremendous benefit to my morale; the tutors, counsellors and administration staff alike gave me every support and encouragement. I really wanted to complete that particular course, which was proving to be the most difficult to date, and wanted my examination result to be a success.

I suppose the feelings that I had about my courses and study was that, if I did not succeed at anything else in life, at least I was progressing in this. If I were to pass my current course, I would be half way to a degree so I was determined to do my best to complete the three courses yet to come. Unnoticed by myself, but commented upon by my friends, was my growing interest in knowledge generally. Comments such as "here comes" Hurley with his bits of paper!' were directed at me, due to my interest in cutting passages from articles and sharing them with everyone else.

It was coming up to exam time and I felt I was doing OK - I had attended a residential school at Canterbury University, where I picked up quite a lot of knowledge. I sat the exam and, as usual, could not judge how well or badly I had done. Eventually, a letter contained my exam result. Thank goodness my postman did his job. I was afraid to open it in case I had failed. I left it unopened for about four hours, then I plucked up enough courage to open it very gently - I had passed. This made me like a child with a new toy - excitement so great that I was charged with all the impetus I needed to beat those depressions, overcome my educationally disadvantaged background, and look forward to further studies.

I decided next on a course called 'Changing Britain, Changing World (Geographical Perspectives)'. The material tackled issues both in Britain and in the context of the wider world. I was being taught to develop an understanding of issues from a geographical point of view. It showed me how geography could be important in understanding how society works, as well as the different trade and commercial relationships between countries. Whilst I did not achieve high marks for the continuing assessment, I did get enough to gain a pass. The tutor was acceptable, but I did not share the same rapport with him as I had with previous course tutors.

October arrived, and with it, time for my examination. I was worried as my continuing assessment marks had been disappointing, and it was with trepidation that I sat the exam. Maybe, fingers crossed, I might just gain a pass.

The now familiar waiting period of long dark weeks leading up to Christmas was made worse by pangs of apprehension. I also had no studying to do until I registered for a new course in the New Year. I got a little depressed, but was determined not to let it beat me. Christmas week arrived and, with it, my examination results. My usual ritual with the envelope occurred and yet I had passed again. This lifted me right out of my depression; there is no doubt that the Open University is one of the best things I have found in my life.

In the New Year of 1987, I registered for a course called 'The State and Society", a political course. My profile of courses was chosen to fill in my lack of knowledge in the areas, and it was very beneficial to me that the Open University does not confine students to one faculty. The course proved to be very interesting, and a fellow student was a blind man with inspiring determination. It did not necessarily follow - but it made me think, why cannot I be more determined with regard to my ailment?

As the year progressed, I maintained a good balance, with no highs and just a few small lows. Thanks to the knowledge and experience I had now gained concerning mood swings, I was becoming more able to manage them. This year the assessment I received about my continuing studies was good, and this was an encouraging omen for the outcome of the exam. The year, overall, was uneventful, just the same old pattern of work at the Post Office.

Autumn arrived, and exam time came again. The weeks prior to it had been stressful, as there was a lot of revision to be done. Whilst one thinks one has done OK, one never knows how an exam will be - it is a case of do it, and then wait and see. Whatever the cause, more and more people seem to experience depression at this time of year. It may be caused by the wet and gloomy weather, 'Seasonal Affective Disorder' (SAD), or by the long dark nights.

I too got a little depressed, but nothing like those lows that used to throw me to the floor. As the end of the year arrived, the excitement and anticipation of learning my exam result was pending. As before, the envelope arrived in Christmas week and yet again, I had the same difficulty in coming to terms with its opening. Eventually the decisive moment: I opened the envelope and the news was good, another pass. I could not have felt better if I had won the Lottery!

In 1988, I registered for my next course, 'Introduction to New Technology'. This was the last course of my degree and I could not believe that I had completed five courses. It may seem that I am blowing my own trumpet here, but the success I had achieved in my studies had been under difficult personal circumstances. All tribute must go to the Open University, who had been so good to me.

Computers and New Technology were both way over my head, so it was just as well that I could attend as many tutorials as possible. I sat at the first tutorial listening to the students talking about hard disks and using incomprehensible jargon. It could have been a mechanic discoursing on clutch brakes as far as I was concerned. I asked myself why I was doing this course. I could have done many easier courses than this....

I suppose I wanted to know about computers and technology, so I had better get on with learning about them. This should stop me having bouts of mood swings. I decided to hire a computer and to demonstrate how ignorant I was I attempted a preliminary exercise. I did not realise the exercise was designed for a one-drive computer. As I had two drives in mine, I rang the tutor and told him I thought I had hired the wrong computer. Fortunately, a fellow student whom I had got to know, and who was very well versed in computers, took me under his wing and taught me a lot. He even took me to his house and gave me lessons on his. I could contact him by phone or e-mail any time I needed to, as nothing was too much trouble for him. I felt so glad that once again such a generous person should befriend me.

I was no longer in awe of my fellow students as I now felt nearly as knowledgeable as they did. Indeed, I think I was more knowledgeable of the philosophy and social part of the course than they were, and this I could attribute to my life-experience as well as to the courses in social sciences that I had already completed.

My studies, even though they were difficult, perhaps particularly because they were difficult, were giving me satisfaction. I felt that I was doing something constructive in my life and this compensated for the menial work at the Post Office. They also contributed significantly to my morale and sense of self-worth.

The year rolled on, and again exam time arrived. This one was the decisive factor - I just had to pass in order to get my degree. As a gambler would say, there was a lot riding on this. To add to my frustration, this was the first time that this type of course was being presented. That is to say the first time that a computing element was part of a course and part of the exam. This meant that students could have conferences and e-mail one another all around the country, and there were observers from different countries assessing the outcomes. I sat the exam and thought I had done well enough to pass. My fellow student, who had been so helpful to me, was doubtful as to how well he had performed. His self-doubts set me back - I started to revise my thoughts - I shall leave things at that.

Christmas week arrived at last and that long-awaited letter bearing the result of my exam arrived with it. I performed my usual act - waited for about four hours to open it. I tried to read the notice through the envelope. I opened it and tried to read it upside down. I thought I could read two 'S's together - this could mean the word is 'PASS'. I turned it the right way up and sure enough, the word is PASS!

I danced on the kitchen table that day, in spite of all my aches and pains. One of my first thoughts was of the words of my first tutor six years ago: 'you are here'. I now knew that I had some brain cells, and that my degree was something that no one could take away from me. Whether I had a disability or not, whether it was mental or physical, I was handicapped. Something has been taken from me. If I achieve an award - that cannot be taken from me.

Into 1989, and the question was - should I register to do my 'Honours' degree? Third level courses are very difficult, and there was not much of a choice. I decided upon a political course called 'Democratic Government and Politics'.

I had to make the choice of attending the ceremony at which degrees are confessed. I did not think that I would go, as I dislike pomp and ceremony. My friend Eamon advised me to attend, and after some deliberation I decided that I would. I found the ceremony and its proceedings very impressive. It was held at the Wembley Conference Centre, the interior of which comprises a large circular arena. The number of guests that attended in support of the graduates impressed me also.

My new studies began in May, and the good thing that arose was the location of the tutorials - face-to-face tuition is very important and one can exchange ideas with fellow students. They were to be held in a study centre at Kings College, near to my work, which meant that I could attend them regularly. As I mentioned before, my supervisor was accommodating and allowed me to take time off, and work time in lieu. I received good marks for the first assignments, which were very encouraging, as the first blocks of this course were difficult, going back to ancient times of Greece and the like. The tutor was a woman and held a doctorate; she was an excellent instructor.

I was, at the same time, suffering from tremors as a result in a change in my Lithium dosage. Unfortunately, they affected my studies and this was reflected in my assignment marks. October came and the dreaded exam time; afterwards I thought I had done reasonably well and now it was a case of waiting to see.

The months passed and it was Christmas time again. My exam results arrived, and this time brought disappointment. I went through my usual letter opening ritual, and I had failed by just four marks. I decided to appeal, as my continuing assessment marks had been very good. It took a month of tension for my papers to be remarked. I decided to register for the 1990 course, called 'Global Politics'.

In January, at the end of the month, the result of my appeal arrives - I had been unsuccessful. This was not a good time for me; it seemed that nothing was in my favour. However, I had commenced studying the new course and later in the year, I would have to revise for the re-sit of last year's exam. I began to think that I should have postponed the re-sit for a year, but on the other hand, perhaps my fortune would improve.

It was coming up to the summer and I had seen my consultant psychiatrist a few times. He had seemed satisfied with my progress and mental state and had suggested changing my Lithium treatment to that of a drug call carbamazepine. He then decided against doing so as the Lithium was working well, and it was getting near the time when I would be attending Summer School for the 'Global Politics' course. I was not in the best of conditions to go and my absence would have been excused. However, the tuition I would receive would be invaluable and, as I would have to sit two exams this year, I really wanted to attend.

The Summer School was held at Warwick University. This was helpful as I had been there before. I planned my route to Warwick very carefully and ensured that I could stop during my journey at least six times. This would prevent me from getting stiff and I could have short breaks from driving. I took my neck braces, which helped ease my neck and shoulders and I managed the journey to Warwick without any trouble. When I arrived, I was shown to my living quarters, which were located on the ground floor, as I had requested. Under the mattress on the bed was a board, which was good for my back. The Open University had placed a board under my mattress ever since my first Summer School and so everything was in place to enable the accommodation of my physical disabilities.

Unfortunately, the library and restaurant were both a long way from my residential accommodation and this gave me a rough time getting around. To make matters worse, in the library it was painful for me to reach up and down the shelves. I got a brain wave by the middle of the week when it seemed that the books had moved ever further away - I would get the books and their location for my research from the computer. Alas, there were no suitable books on the computer, and it was not programmed to suit me. All of these frustrations were beginning to get me down and I started to think that everyone else was making great progress - I was the only one in a mess. I had swapped my shoes for a pair of slippers as my feet were swelling.

One day I went to see a counsellor to get some indication of what I could do if I passed my 'Honours' Degree. He mentioned to me that I seemed depressed and so I told him what I was enduring that week, and something of my history. He said that he would have a word with the course director and, between them, they would sort things out, so that my time there would be more comfortable and an aid to my studies.

The following day when I was in the library, a man came up to me and introduced him self. He was the course director. He told me to carry on as best I could, and that between now and exam time, if I experienced any difficulty that I should contact him. He would also arrange for special tuition for me. With regard to my mood swings, he said that the Open University had tutors who were also affected by these. This was of great consolation to me and I thanked him sincerely for coming to see me. Our conversation gave a great boost to my confidence - I felt like a different person and when I went for a cup of tea during a break, I met up with a couple. We began talking and, for some reason, I started to tell them about myself and my mood swings. They were so intrigued by my tale that we soon became engrossed in conversation and missed the last two-hour tutorial!

The following day I continued to feel better and was determined to make the best of things. All the negative feelings I had experienced earlier in the week had dissipated and I began to enjoy myself. I socialised with fellow students, and a number of them were sensitive when I had the courage to tell them about my mood swings. One girl told me that her father was a manic-depressive and this was again consoling - so little was known and understood of my condition by apparently unaffected people.

I felt I had achieved a positive outcome through attending the Summer School. The journey home was much easier than I feared, as I made regular stops. The tension I had experienced on the journey to Warwick was not there on the way back.

I now had a lot of studying to do and only a couple of months left in which to do it. I had an assignment of three thousand words to complete on the research I had carried out at the Summer School to finalise. The expiry date for submitting it was just a few weeks away - I completed the draft and it looked good. I did not have to type the essay, but I felt that this would improve its presentation. It would not improve the content, but the appearance. I arranged with a friend to type it for me, but in the event she could not do so in time, and I became annoyed about this. (I did not know that at this time I had become a little high since seeing the course director at the Summer School).

Eventually I found someone else to type it for me. I put a lot of good effort into the revision for the re-sit of my exam and for the current course. I attended a couple of tutorials for both and I received the results of my final assessment - a mark of 60% - that really cheered me up. I was apprehensive, not satisfied with a degree, I had to have those 'Honours'. To think that before attending the Open University, there had never been a passing thought for me concerning self-improvement - there were now times when I had to pinch myself to believe that this was truly happening to me.

Now there was that added self-induced pressure - I had to succeed. This was in part because there were two wonderful people supporting my efforts - Chris Youle and Bonita Thompson, both Open University Senior Counsellors. There are not enough superlatives in the English language to describe their goodness to me. My success had been their reward for all the effort they in turn made for me. I know I was a nuisance to them, as when I was high I wrote all sorts of funny letters to them. I also had the habit of phoning them with hair-brained ideas at unsocial times. Nonetheless, they were marvellous in dealing with my swinging mental states and were most sympathetic to my physical disabilities. It became important to gain my 'Honours' just to repay Chris and Bonita.

Getting back to studying, exam time arrived and I sat for both of the exams - the current course exam and the re-sit. I thought afterwards that I had done just well enough to pass both. It has been said that when high, a person has great insight into different subjects, a kind of extra intelligence and superiority in their perception. This, if true, would have been of immense value to me when doing exams. In the next few months, the arthritis also worsened and was extremely painful.

Christmas week finally arrived and with it, the exam results. I put the small envelope, which contained them into a large one and gave it all to Eamon to be opened after Christmas had passed - I just could not cope with the envelope opening ritual at that time.

Christmas over, I decided to see the results of my two 'Honours' exams. Apprehension multiplied by a factor of ten could not describe how I felt. This time I looked at the envelope for ten minutes, then with a swift movement of the hand I opened the envelope and, *YES, I HAD PASSED BOTH COURSES. I HAD ACHIEVED THE BA HONS! In addition, how proud of myself I was.*

This moment in my life far exceeded any other. Because of my mood swings, I had always felt that I was inferior to other people, but now I had an Honours degree and no one could take that away from me. The words of Charles Stewart Parnell, the great Englishman of Irish politics came to my mind. 'No man has the right to halt the march of a nation. No man has the right to say this far shall you go and no further.'

Nineteen ninety had been an otherwise bad year for me, and achieving passes in both courses was a brilliant recompense.

1991

It was now 1991 and my studies were complete. I was at a loose end. The Open University has been like a family to me. The tutors, administrative staff and everyone connected to it have all been so good to me. They had all shared great understanding and expertise when dealing with people, and in my case, had understood mood swings very well. This made a tremendous difference to me and made my life far easier. With regard to my arthritis, they made allowances for me, in allowing my assignments come in later than the deadline. They had given me a flexi writer to make it easier for my hands when writing. When I first suffered from arthritis, a tutor counsellor came to visit me. At two Summer Schools, I saw the course directors concerning my ailments. Due to disc trouble and arthritis in my back, each Summer School ensured that a board was put under my mattress to alleviate the pain.

With regard to the therapeutic side of things, The Open University studies were invaluable to my mental well-being and for my morale. Whilst it was difficult at times, especially as my educational background was disadvantaged, studying also kept me from worrying about my pains and aches. My psychiatrist and GP were encouraging and supportive too. I missed not having a course to do that year. Luckily, looking around to find one occupied my time. I thought that I was not qualified to do any other degree, and I looked at many different syllabuses trying to find something that would fit - the search seemed to be of no avail and I was disappointed.

Then I came across a brochure for Commerce and Industry. Management, Manufacture and Technology courses were available through the Open University. The discovery of these gave me a lift, and something to look forward to. I thought that these were probably way above my head as I had worked in accounts departments for most of my life. Whilst I had worked in industry in Ireland before leaving for England, it would have moved on since that time and would now be much more sophisticated.

I decided to visit the Open University Regional Offices in London as I wished to meet the Senior Tutor in Technology. Unfortunately, he was not available, but I did get to see a Senior Science Tutor, George Loveday - a most accommodating person. We looked at the Management, Manufacture and Technology course and it seemed that this might be a better shot. Mr Loveday said I would need to do a computing course before attempting this and picked one out for me. He also told me how to go about getting financial help to for the fees for the computing course. It was a good day's work; I now had the means to do the course, something tangible to aim for.

The start of the New Year 1992 had arrived. I registered for the Computers and Computing course with the Open University. It was nearly twelve months since I had had a drink. If I had a friend to visit, or if I went to someone's house, then I maybe had one drink. At the advice of my consultant, I began a diet. If I could shed a few pounds, it would take some weight off my joints, which in turn would alleviate the pain from the arthritis. Once again, I would like to say that the year was kinder to me than it might have been. Eamon had died, but somehow I picked myself up, and with support from the right sources, did quite well. I am sure that my good friend was up there in heaven praying for me.

Into 1992, and I had my new course to look forward to. It started in February and at first it came as a shock - the course was more difficult that I had anticipated. There was some slight consolation in the realisation that the other students were equally perturbed. One of them had to drop out. A couple of fellow students and me got together and tried to work out the problems between us. Another student, Paul, and I continued to work together. At no stage when it got tough did I ever harbour any doubts about persevering with it - one thing I knew for sure, there would be no time for mood swings! The course demanded so much concentration that there was no space for the highs and lows.

Even though the computing course was difficult, I was achieving average marks in my assignments. I was visiting Paul's house sometimes to study; he knew so much about computers, although the course was proving demanding for him as well. We worked well together and achieved some good results. Sometimes Clarice, Paul's wife, would invite me to stay for a meal. They were very nice people, and even though I had known them for just a short while it seemed like a lifelong friendship.

At this time I used to visit my friend Denis Treacy, seeing him once or twice a week, appreciating being able to talk to him. He was someone who understood me. I would often say to him 'if I am boring shut me up'. Denis would read my assignments for the Open University and always gave me great encouragement. I think that others reassurance has been very important for my studies.

Autumn was on its way and therefore it was time for the run up to the annual examination routine. There was an optional Residential School available to Computing course students, which was being held at Aston University. Paul and I decided to go, as we would greatly benefit from the tuition. It was a very intense course and we did indeed learn a lot.

Time passed and it was now October. The day of the examination was approaching fast. Paul was very apprehensive and since I thought that Paul was a lot more advantaged than I, what chance of success did I have? We sat the exam, and I thought that I might just have scraped a pass mark. Paul himself did not think that he had done at all well; in fact he felt that he had performed badly. I tried to console myself by commenting to myself that Paul had high personal goals and standards, and when he does not achieve them, he gets despondent. In my own optimistic way, I figured out that Paul had passed and that this would also put me in there with a chance. The next few months passed quietly. I was considering the course that I might take next year. All of the options appeared daunting, and they were expensive as well, which meant I would have to apply for some grants.

As in previous years, the examination results arrived during Christmas week. For once, I was not worried if I had passed or not - at least I had gained enough experience to undertake the forthcoming courses. As I opened the letter containing the results, it struck me that it would be nice to pass after all the hard work. Then the thrill came, I had passed - what a confidence boost. By passing this computing course, I had acquired the knowledge to study the next courses. I immediately telephoned Paul, and he had passed as well, just as I had thought. He was, however, disappointed that he had not done better. I knew how deeply I was in his debt, as he had contributed so much to my success.

The year began quietly and as my studies would not commence until November, I had plenty of time to select a course. I needed all the courage I could muster to tackle any one of these courses, and I would need to pass four in order to gain a diploma. On passing the diploma, a major project has to be presented in order to gain a Masters. I had no notion of reaching that stage, but the prospect was one that I considered and felt its presence there in front of me.

Returning to 1993; it was almost autumn, and with it came the commencement of my Open University course. It had been difficult to arrive at a decision, being aware that these post-graduate courses are difficult; I decided to select a fifteen-point course, as this would test me. If I could cope with this, I would be competent to handle the other courses - I would find out if I had the ability to pass post-graduate courses. I would have preferred to have studied a thirty-point course, as this would have made the cost of the overall diploma less expensive.

The course began in November, and we had an induction session. This was the only face-to-face meeting we would have, as the rest of the course was conducted like a correspondence course, with access to one's tutor by telephone or e-mail. The induction was most satisfactory and I was pleased to be on board - with one exception. I anticipated that the mathematics element would be a problem.

There was a nice surprise at the end of the meeting when I learned that the course had just been upgraded to a thirty-point course. This put a different complexion on the diploma, as I needed four thirty point courses, i.e. one hundred and forty points, to gain the diploma. Furthermore a fifteen-point course would have cost almost as much as a thirty pointer. The economics of this for me was that I must find the cheapest route possible. Should I, by any chance, survive and pass my Masters, it would have cost me about £10,000. A lot of money to prove that I have some grey matter in that thick skull of mine!

I wrote off for grants with no success; it was a waste of time and energy. However, I did receive £400 from Arthritis Care, and Chris Yule, Senior Tutor/Counsellor at the Open University obtained £200 for me. God bless them both!

I imagine that many people had expectations of 1994, and I was no exception. The start of the year began and I was doing the usual things - visiting my GP, psychiatric unit and attending The Fellowship meetings. My studies were progressing exceptionally well; I achieved a very good mark for my second assignment and, over the next few months, this continued to be the case. The examination for the course was scheduled to take place in May. After I had taken it, my feelings were a little mixed - I was unsure whether I would pass. There had been one question, which I had thought was too easy - maybe I had interpreted it incorrectly. I now had to wait until July for the result.

I had registered for another course, 'Implementation of New Technologies', which commenced immediately after the exam. My first assignment for this course was not a good one - luckily it was not assessed. I was very disappointed, and told myself that I would have to do better.

Along came July and the result of my exam. The postman delivered at 8am. It was 1 p.m. when I decided to open the envelope. I was down by the river enjoying one of my favourite spots when I began the customary opening ritual - looking through the window, trying to see the result, then tearing it open slowing to gently get at the result. The result appeared - I had passed. It may seem childish, but each time a positive exam result came, it represented another breakthrough and personal achievement. It was a postgraduate course, which had been difficult, and although it remained a long way away, it was one step further towards gaining my Masters Degree. Studying has had a profound influence upon my life and has given me a sense of purpose. The environment, tutors and administrative staff at the Open University have all been very good to me.

I started the next course at the end of May. This course I had to withdraw from when I suffered a heart attack. The studying kept me occupied and helped to pass the time. It was now August, and I had received two very good results for my first two assignments. This gave me the encouragement I needed to persevere. Around this time, I received a communiqué from the Heart Support Group who held their meetings in the local hospital every month. It was attended by ex-patients who had experienced heart attacks or surgery. I went along (as I mentioned before, I do not get about much socially) and was glad that I accepted their invitation; on my first night they had a very good speaker, and further guests and activities were lined up for the future.

My course exam came along in October. *Prior to sitting the exam, I had three forms to complete but I could not write, due to tremors in my hand - a side effect of the medication interacting. In the exam, I waited a few minutes until things calmed down, and then tried to write fish and chips half a dozen times. This got me settled and I was able to commence the exam paper, but it had disturbed my concentration, and afterwards had an adverse effect upon me for the rest of the time.*

I commenced another course in November - 'Manufacturing and Management'. Christmas week arrived with the result of my exam. The usual ritual was observed before I was finally able to read the result. I had failed by two marks and was entitled to a re-sit. I decided to appeal, as I thought I might not have made the Open University sufficiently aware of the trembling incident that had occurred at the exam. The appeal was unsuccessful - they had taken into account the episode of my tremors when marking my exam.

The New Year of 1996 arrived. With the coming of this year, I began to suddenly feel my age. Maybe it was because I felt I had been deprived of many things, due to my mood swings. Often when the going gets rough, I repeat to myself 'why me?' Only those that experience mood swings can know how alone one can be at times. It is probably because of this that I like to spend time by the River Thames every day. There is something tranquil and serene about water.

The result of the first assignment I gave in for the Manufacture and Management course arrived. I had not achieved a good result - luckily the rating for this assignment was not significant. For the first time, I had a tutor with whom I had no rapport. I also had a visit to the psychiatrist in March, when it was revealed that my Lithium level might be affecting my thyroid gland - this meant a reduction in my Lithium intake.

A couple of weeks passed and the fun started - I went sky high. I received the result of a second assignment, again a poor result. I was very upset and rang the Open University. The girl who spoke to me knew me, and of my mood swings and she was terrific in handling me. She said that she would arrange for my tutor to be replaced and for the assignment to be re-marked. My reaction when she wanted me to send the marked assignment back was, to me, wholly justifiable. I argued that an unmarked script be assessed, and was most insistent that that was the way it should be done.

Afterwards I was sorry for my attitude, as the girl had tried to be so fair and helpful. Something similar happened with my psychiatrist. His office was supposed to ring me with an appointment. When that did not happen, I got into a rage and went to see my doctor. I wanted my psychiatrist changed. My doctor, who knew me very well, tried to appease me. Eventually I agreed to leave things for a few days.

I have noticed that when I am high, I become extremely dogmatic. An attitude develops; no one dare question my authority. On both of these occasions, I changed my attitude fairly quickly and all was resolved within a couple of days. I got a new tutor, my assignment was re-marked and my GP obtained a new appointment for me with the psychiatrist. Upon seeing the psychiatrist, he increased my Lithium to its original dose.

About a month passed, and my high began to decline. I felt drained - I had been rushing around during this period, feeling that I wanted to do everything at the same time. A couple of months passed and I received some good results from my new tutor - my relationship with him was going well. My exam would take place in a couple of weeks' time and, in spite of this bad patch, I thought I was well prepared. Then, having sat the exam (as so often is my reaction) I was not sure that I had answered the questions properly. However, I thought that I had done well enough to pass.

In July I received the result of my exam. This time, my ritual was different. On the outside of the envelope was the message, 'do not bend', and since we got a certificate with each course, I thought that this time they had put it in with the results. This meant I had passed. When I opened the envelope, to my disappointment I found I had failed by four marks. Again, I had the option of doing the exam in October or May of the following year, 1997. I opted for May as I already had a re-sit in October. I seemed to be up to my eyes in them.

I started to revise for my October re-sit. I wanted to make sure that I passed this exam. When visiting the psychiatrist, we discussed my moving house and mutually agreed that it would be better for me if I did not have to negotiate stairs. My GP also thought that it would be a good idea. In August, I visited the rheumatology department and it was decided to change some of my medication. Two tablets a week would replace forty-two tablets, all of which I had been taking regularly since I had left hospital. I had been taking, on average, eighteen tablets a day and as I was also taking sleeping tablets since my heart attack.

I sometimes worried that the mood swings were causing my sleeplessness. Not being able to sleep is a sure sign of going high. I was relieved when I discovered it was my arthritis that was the cause. Its pain was causing me to wake up. The rheumatology specialist arranged for me to see the sister in charge to monitor my condition.

I went to a residential school at Reading University to prepare for my exam. This was the first time I had driven such a long distance since my heart attack. I was just gradually getting my confidence back. Even though the course was very intense, I thoroughly enjoyed it. It was good to mix with the other students, some of whom were working in industry and were being sponsored by their respective companies. I had no such support. I was pleased that I had been able to drive to Reading and back. October arrived, and the day of my exam. Having sat it I thought I had done well, although perhaps there had been one question I could have done better.

Some prospective buyers came to view my house. I had planned to go away for Christmas, but this would not be possible it there were to be a sale. I received a couple of offers for the house, but neither came near my reserve. The end of November came and at last, I received a decent offer, which I readily accepted. I then had to find a suitable new home for myself. Even though I had arranged to stay with friends, I was anxious about how long it might take me to find the place that would suit me.

Within three weeks, I was successful and it was in the same area in which I had lived for so long. I still had the chance to go away for Christmas but could not pursue it in case contracts might have had to be signed. Christmas week came and so did the result of my exam. I had my usual envelope opening ritual. To my surprise the result read 'pending'. I was confused at this and rang the Open University office. Clare, a very capable person, explained it to me. I had passed but would have to have a Vive Voce, an oral test, as this would confirm my grading. It would take the form of an interview, and at the end of her explanation, Clare gave me the phone number for the examinations department - they in turn confirmed what she had told me.

If I had not been so excited and had read the letter properly, I could have deduced the answer myself. Anyway, this information cheered me up immensely and my Christmas was better on account of it. I now had passed two courses out of three. If I could pass the third course I would be well on my way to a diploma; I had built my life around studying and I knew that my life would have been different had I received a good education when I had been young. I also knew that it would have influenced the course of my life regardless of mood swings.

After my move, and the settling in to my new house, I returned to preparing for my re-sit. I badly wanted to pass both courses and I had decided that I would withdraw from my degree if I failed. It would have been too expensive to continue, having failed these courses. In March, the psychiatrist discovered that my thyroid gland was again playing up. He reduced my Lithium dosage and after a few weeks, I began to go low. This was the opposite of the previous effect of reducing my Lithium, when I had gone high. The psychiatrist put me back on the original dose. He thought about putting me on carbamazepine but I declined to do so. I guess you could say, 'if it ain't broke, don't fix it!' Lithium had worked well for me, and if I could get over a few hitches, I would be OK again.

A few weeks passed and the depression began to lift. I went to Reading University for a residential course and this was beneficial as I was able to converse with students who were actually working in the field. I was working from a theoretical point of view, and to exchange ideas and working practice with engineers and scientists was very helpful. The course was very intense but also very enjoyable.

The day of the exam arrived at the end of April, and afterwards, I thought I had made a fairly good job of it, hopefully good enough to pass. Then there was the long wait until July for the result. The results arrived in the middle of the month and, naturally, I was excited. I broke with tradition that time and opened the envelope after ten minutes. Admittedly, this was done very slowly and with my eyes half closed. I glanced down the letter and my eyes suddenly gazed on the word pass, and arthritis or no, I did a little jig!

I have outlined my studies blow by blow, and hope that this has not been too laboured. It does illustrate what a marvellous therapy and an outlet it has been for me. I know that I would go without a great many things, in order to be educated. Something else, which I would like to say, and which may sound corny but is also true, is that two doctors have told me quite independently that I have a hunger for knowledge. Maybe this is the source of my endeavours.

8. Breakthrough

I will begin with what was a very poignant time of my life, when I was attending what was then known as the Marriage Guidance Council. I had mentioned some relationships I had been involved with, and other aspects of my life. On my third visit, the counsellor asked me if I thought there might be something wrong with my personality. This seemed to strike a chord - sometimes I had thought that I indeed might be different from everybody else. The counsellor suggested that I should give it some thought and we would discuss it at our next meeting.

Prior to attending the Marriage Guidance counselling sessions, I had been researching and analysing my depressive state with no success. Suddenly it came to me that it was not only depression I suffered from - there had been phases in my life when I thought I was extra happy. Now, on reflection, I could, for the first time, recall these elated states. The recollection was unclear, but I could recognise that at times, depressions followed periods of high elation.

Drinking patterns also began to emerge in relation to the swings up and down. I was normally a social drinker, with an average intake of a few drinks. Sometimes I might exceed this, but not to any great degree. When I was high, I felt so good I drank as though each day would be the last. My friends would kid me over this, saying that they could not tell where I put it all. It did not alarm them or they would have made further comment. On the other hand, when depressed, I felt insignificant. I would not want to go out and would not touch alcohol at all. There was the fear that I did not want to be in the company of others.

It is difficult to describe the lack of inhibition that a high brings; you think that everyone is your friend. Being Irish, or belonging to a small community, this

82

would probably be the case, but certainly not in a city such as London.

During the counselling I was continuing to research my condition. In a small way, I guess I had been trying to investigate it right from the first episode. What did become clear was that focusing on depression for all these years had been misleading. I read about John Ogden, the famous pianist who suffered from depression, but mood swings were not mentioned. Then I read about Winston Churchill; he used to call depression 'the black dog'. He also drank quite a lot at times, and for me, there was a parallel in this. Graham Greene was another famous depressive whom I read about - he went for up to twelve months without writing, due to his suffering.

I began to recognise two personalities in myself, and perhaps sometimes other people might have noticed these traits too. Friends who are close to me, and have always known me to be contrary, might not recognise this split personality. The drinking might disguise what would otherwise be a misdemeanour and a cause of discontent. Elated states sometimes produced artificial arrogance, due to a false sense of high intelligence. (It is a pity that some aspects of that state cannot be extracted and put to good use).

On my fourth counselling session we discussed what I had found out, and agreed that in a relationship I could appear to be in different moods at different periods of time. I had never seen things this way before - it would have presented problems for any partner. Furthermore, I presented a different personality at the in-between stages, halfway between a high and a low.

Then there were the stable periods, when I had a 'normal' personality. It seemed I was revealing five personalities within me. They could be described as moods, but mood affects personality, and there was no doubt that there were personality changes of a

83

particular kind. It could be argued that most people experience mood swings, but not as pronounced as mine. I thanked the counsellor profoundly for her help and advice - I felt a much wiser person and far better equipped to deal with the cause and affect of my condition. The great mystery of my life was beginning to unravel itself.

At this time, 1985, I saw a television programme about manic depression. Clare Rayner presented it, and I heard those words for the first time. I related to the man who was the subject of the programme - some of his actions and moods were much like mine. He was a professional man, a barrister, and the extreme moods he experienced affected his ability to practice - he lost everything he had as a result.

At the end of the documentary, details about the Manic Depressive Fellowship were given, such as how you could contact the organisation. The programme enlightened me so much I lost no time in contacting the Fellowship. I obtained a list of group meetings, and the venues where they were held. I opted for a Barnes venue and went along one evening shortly afterwards. There were about a dozen people there, men and women. They made me feel at home at once and explained what the meeting was about and how the Fellowship intended to help its members and others with whom it came into contact. I was told that I did not have to speak if I did not want to, particularly if I felt low or depressed, and at the end of the meeting I felt so comforted and impressed.

It is hard to describe the feeling of satisfaction brought about by knowing that there were others whom suffered from this affliction. The meeting itself was carried out in an informal manner and had the air of being a somewhat social occasion. I was also impressed by the attendance of partners; those who care. As manic-depressives can cause so much disruption to their partner's lives, to attend the meetings helped them to learn how to survive. This first meeting proved very informative to me. To be in the company of others lumbered with the same illness brought untold comfort to what had been a life long state of feeling marginalised.

I attended a second meeting of the Fellowship, which was held a fortnight later. There were a number of new faces and some from the last meeting were absent. I was told that this was a trend, people coming and going. The Fellowship had not been established for very long and was by nature peripatetic, being held in people's homes for want of a permanent venue.

The bi-polar aspect of manic depression was becoming increasingly recognisable as I listened to other people's accounts of their illness. Whilst I use the word illness here, it was not acknowledged as such until the mid-1980s. In my own case, the first acknowledgement came through my counselling visits. The Fellowship allowed me to switch my focus to the highs. I could see a six-year pattern emerging. A high would be followed approximately three months later by a low, a depression. I could now understand the words that nurse had spoken so many years ago, 'You could sell your house and give away all your money and possessions'. Now I know that I am a mood swinger, I hope I can deal with it better, both cause and effect on myself and on those around me.

One thing I now recognise is that my lows were magnified due to the elatedness of the highs. I did not recognise the artificial confidence and exuberance experienced during a high and therefore, the awfulness of the lows, which could not be reconciled. This would make me feel worse, and would aggravate the effects of depression. "What is dragging me down so far? A few weeks ago I was at ease with the world - why has it gone so devastatingly wrong?"

Now, however, I become more informed. Through hearing other people's accounts at the Fellowship meetings, a learning process was taking place within me and I began to understand that there is no fixed pattern to mood swings. There is no knowing whether it may or may not happen again. I tried not to go too deeply into their analysis - it would have been of no great help to me.

I would not have told people openly about my mood swings. I was able to analyse them - not an easy task, I discovered as time went on. It was on the one hand easy for me to recognise the lows, and I could determine the degree of their depth. The trouble lay in the highs, and my ability to determine what degree of elation I had reached. The other trait of manic depression, that of not being able to sleep was rearing its ugly head again, and all during this period I could not sleep. During insomniac times, I would get up and do some studying for a couple of hours. That pleased me - I could turn unproductive time not sleeping, into productive time studying. It was better for me to do this than to lie in bed worrying about things. Whether it was because of my moods or otherwise, I have always had a dislike of wasting time.

My hours of work at the Post Office interfered with my attendance of the Fellowship meetings, and I did not go to any during 1986. This period was disappointing, but was recompensed in part by a quarterly magazine which was distributed to members, and which gave a lot of news and information. I had made friends with Alan Mitchell, the chairman of the Fellowship, and his wife Margaret. On any occasion when I had a problem or needed a chat, they were very willing to help. They were co-founders of the Fellowship, and Margaret had been a long time sufferer, which had given Alan a great insight into manic depression. He knew more about the condition than most of the psychiatrists I had encountered!

Manic depressives are prime cases for suicide - the pain of life in a depression is so acute that all rationality goes out the window, and a terrible darkness overtakes one.

I had received a couple of invitations for Christmas lunch. I declined them all, deciding instead to have a quiet time on my own. I thought I needed to take stock, and to try to unwind. When I am high, it's like being in another gear - I want to do three or four things at the same time. If I am having a meal and someone telephones me, I do not think twice about talking for hours and letting the meal go cold. Then I would just throw my meal in the waste bin without giving it a second thought.

On the other hand, I might be oblivious of the time, and thus might telephone someone at the most inopportune time. This does not make you a popular person, and makes the telephone bill rather steep. I was unaware sometimes that I was telephoning long distance and abroad, and spent a considerable time on the line. Christmas enabled me to take it easy for a couple of weeks. Eamon visited me a few times, and we went out for a couple of drinks. This diversion, and having the time to talk with Eamon, had a good effect upon me - I could feel myself returning to 'normal'.

The fact that I knew about highs and lows had helped me on this occasion. The pattern that I had been used to, that is a low followed by a high every five or six years, had changed. The years were about right, but this time the highs were not followed by the lows. I could control the highs better through recognition. I am a perfectionist in all that I do, and this may have been at the nub of the problem - this is another trait of the mood swinger.

I started doing voluntary work for the Fellowship. This, I felt, was giving the Fellowship back something in return for what it have given me. It was growing, and hopefully in time it would make an impact on society.

Groups such as this were invaluable and were beginning to be established all over the country. The Fellowship's quarterly magazine, appropriately named Pendulum, contained valuable articles, helpful information and contacts. The voluntary work was therapeutic for me, and took the place of my studies.

A fundamental truth had been revealed to me - whilst I was living one life. I was like two different people with two different and inexplicable mood states.

9. Incarceration

Incarceration 1 - Shenley Mental Hospital -1964

I had been petrified by the events that had occurred following my attempted suicide. Having not known where I was being taken, I arrived at Shenley, where I found the atmosphere morbid and the patients frightening. In my whole life, I had never been so scared - in retrospect it would have challenged the mettle of anyone. I was taken to the admissions ward, where there were all categories of patients. Lack of information was making me nervous and frustrated.

Looking back, I thought someone could have given me some outline of what was happening to me, or was this 'not knowing' to be the punishment for what I had done? It seemed similar to the treatment given to prisoners. For a week, I could not sleep and sat at night with the nurses for company. Not a great consolation, but at least they enjoyed a warm open fire.

The patients terrified me, I was terribly depressed and wondered if I was going to be violent and aggressive just like them. How could I have been expected to cope with the threatening atmosphere around me? I felt like someone on remand whose case had not yet been tried, and someone who might not be guilty at all. In any place of rehabilitation, I would expect a doctor to explain to the patient the likely course of treatment or how rehabilitation would proceed - at Shenley, silence ruled.

At night, some of the patients were locked up, more or less with their own consent. I did not know at that time that mood swingers are a bigger danger to themselves than to others. As I write this, I still am inclined to think and say the word prisoner, instead of patient. One morning, I was asked to help the nurses with a man who had come into the ward having been stabbed. It was unclear as to whether he had inflicted the wound himself, or whether he had been attacked, but he was in a bad way. Somehow this had an effect upon me - even though I was scared out of my wits, being able to help made me feel positive - a good omen, given the hell of the past weeks.

I plucked up enough courage to write to the company secretary of my new employer. I had been there for just two weeks, and now had to try to explain my behaviour. He replied, requesting that my psychiatrist write to him. The letter was sent, although I do not know its contents. I received a second letter, saying that the post to which I had been appointed was still mine and, although no sick pay could be given to me due to the short term of employment, my job was intact and waiting for me when I could return.

What a fillip that letter was, and what a considerate employer to have me back after such a short acquaintance. I did not realise then how important this gesture was - it was my lifeline and triggered me onto the road to recovery. To this day, I appreciate the wonderful kindness of this man.

I was moved upstairs to another ward, which was a small improvement on the one I had been in since my admission, although perhaps I was becoming acclimatised. No explanation was given as to why I had been moved. I felt awful and wanted to have ECT treatment, as it had worked for me before. Instant cures are not available, but at times such as these, one gets to believe in miracles.

ECT was not prescribed, and I began to think I would remain there forever. My psychiatrist decided to set up a different form of therapy. This consisted of meetings attended by about a dozen patients, a charge nurse accompanied by another nurse and occasionally attended by the psychiatrist himself.

The meetings were informal; when we plucked up the courage; we spoke of our troubles and how we felt.

It took me a while to speak, as even in a 'normal' situation it is difficult to speak in a gathering of relative strangers. In my state of mind, it was like trying to pull the words out with a crowbar. Amazingly, as time went on, I did improve. It was having a good effect upon me; the quicksand was getting a little firmer and I was beginning to draw myself up to the surface. I began woodworking classes, not keen at first and forcing myself to attend, but I thought they would be therapeutic.

After three weeks, I was allowed back into civilization. I really felt my world was changing for the better. As I walked into Radlett, a journey of roughly two miles, I found the surroundings lovely. Oh to capture that moment again; feelings of complete doom transformed into feelings of joy because of the countryside. To me the fields seemed so green and the air intoxicating.

My first day in the community went well. I was then allowed out for weekends, and on the first of these, one of my closest friends, Hugh, came to collect me. On the weekends that followed I was invited to parties and resumed drinking six or seven pints of beer on occasion. A number of weekends passed in this fashion and then I was informed that I was not supposed to take alcohol. I complied at once when told this, and it did not present a problem.

One day I had a great surprise, although at first I was in a state of embarrassment. A gentleman was walking down the ward. I wished the ground would swallow me up or that I could hide somewhere. The gentleman was the Chairman of a badminton club, which I had joined. It turned out he had indeed come to see me - he had come across my name in the course of his work, which included sports facilities for hospitals. As we spoke I became more at ease and he put my mind at rest. He promised to visit me again and, true to his word, within a week he returned, accompanied by his wife. We went out to one of the village pubs and had a nice evening. No alcohol, just ginger beer, although it might have looked like whisky!

On the couples' next visit, they brought me a beautiful present from members of the badminton club. Such kindness boosted my morale and made me think that I was not such a bad person after all. I became aware of contradiction in others' reactions to me, and some of my friends did not want to visit me. I was both ashamed and embarrassed of seeing anyone. Besides the stigma, there seems to be a gruesome air about mental institutions, for both visitor and patient alike.

My stay in hospital did have some good points. I had become quite friendly with one of the occupational therapists, who was really good to me. The presence of a 'normal' person and their advice was to be relished in a place such as this. I had also developed a rewarding friendship with a fellow patient. This chap had an electrical shop in St Albans and I was permitted to accompany him to the shop a couple of days a week. He stayed in hospital overnight and went to attend to his business every day.

No questions were asked and no information was given - puzzling. I still did not know what my illness was - I thought I was suffering from depression. The problem was that the illness had not been diagnosed in mental health terms at that time. If I had known then what I was suffering from, perhaps I could have dealt with it better.

This is where all the 'ifs' come into play. In hindsight, many things might have seemed different if I had only known... I take the medical profession off the hook; maybe they at that stage did not know either. The frustration for me was when someone was rolling around the floor - I wanted to know if I would be like that. Unless one is in that situation, it cannot be understood how awful the fear and anxiety feel. Then, mental health was a low priority with the politicians of any denomination or party. It never made it into a party manifesto, not even to the slightest extent.

My stay at Shenley was coming to an end. I was getting ready to go back to London and return to 'civilization'. A short while ago this outcome could not have been seen as remotely possible.

Incarceration 2 – Springfield - 1973

Having arrived at Springfield from Charing Cross Hospital, my first impression of its appearance did nothing to raise my morale or take away my blues. It was old and antiquated, the ideal setting for an Alfred Hitchcock film. When one is feeling depressed, morbid surroundings appear much worse. The patients were such a mixed bunch and made me wonder what exactly is wrong with me? I was not given any information as to what was wrong, or what would be happening to me. This was the same for all the patients. Therefore, being in this strange place and starved of information added to my frustration. Sometimes, I thought maybe I deserved nothing better; it was so difficult to put any clear thoughts together.

The ward was of mixed sexes and divided into two sections. The day's routine was entirely structured. Out of bed at 6.30am; breakfast at 8.00am, then 'Conversation Therapy' for the whole ward at 10am. At 11am, the patients went off to their respective therapeutic activities, such as cooking, sewing, woodwork and bookkeeping. 12.30pm was lunchtime, and after lunch, back to therapeutic activities until 5.30pm. There was a tea break during the afternoon. Dinner was served at 6pm followed by a long evening. Some of the patients watched television, while others played cards. If you were really lucky you might have some visitors. At 9pm most went to bed. I forget to mention - drugs and medication were distributed at meal times and at bedtime.

I went to bed every night with the hope that I would not wake up in the morning. To the non-sufferer this may be difficult to understand, but to the affected it's like being in a quagmire with no way out. Struggling out of bed is like conquering Beeches Brook in the Grand National. There are many hurdles to be encountered during the day, but getting out of bed is the major one. I sat there under all sorts of tensions until breakfast arrived - not appetising, but edible. Then, if you were unlucky enough to be on the day's rota for washing up, all those greasy pots and pans were there to cheer you up. There was a rota system, whereby some patients do the washing up after each meal for one week. Whilst unpleasant as a task, it at least forces you through the motions of the day.

The conversation, or group, therapy in the morning I found to be ineffective, as the group was too large, taking in the whole ward. I had the feeling that the numbers attending intimidated patients. I most certainly was discomfited and, even if I had possessed my full faculties, I still could not have spoken to this large congregation.

As I mentioned earlier, I had undergone therapy in Shenley Hospital with a group of twelve, including doctors and nurses, which proved to be successful. However, each hospital has its own way of working. I went to the woodwork room each day for therapy. I did not feel like doing anything. If I simply took a saw and cut a piece of timber, this was an achievement. I did not receive much attention or tutoring; I was more or less left to my own devices. This was a pity, as with a little guidance and encouragement there could have been a chance that the depression might have lifted a little.

The long days were followed by even longer evenings. Of course, I had a number of visitors in the evenings that were very good to me. At times, I felt ashamed of myself - I did not deserve their attention. I was now saddled with a guilt complex to add to my depression. My feelings were that I had let everyone down, and I could see no way out of the dark hole I had fallen into. My uncle, to whom I was close, came to see me at least five out of seven days a week and I genuinely appreciated his visits. One notable lack of care or interest was that of my brother and sister in Ireland - from neither did I receive one line of a letter. I was lucky to have such caring and understanding friends here in London.

I was still not receiving any feedback from the medical staff as to the nature of my condition. As far as I was concerned, I was depressed. Had there been an indication that I was a mood swinger; it would have placed my condition in a different context. For one thing, it would have rid me of that guilt complex. It would probably also have helped me to cope with depression. Had I known that my mental condition was bipolar, it would have given me something to work on. As it was, the one thing I knew, and what bothered me, was my inability to handle depression. There is a cliché that says 'everyone gets depressed and gets over it'. This rang in my ears continuously. It had little relevance to me; as far as I was concerned the difference between the two was like the analogy of the molehill to the mountain. All of this is seen in hindsight. I did not have this knowledge then. Criticism of the medical staff isn't the issue - little about the condition was known at the time.

Returning to life on the ward, nearly every day one of the patients would throw a tantrum. For an hour or two, it would be a noisy mayhem with a patient shouting and rolling around on the floor. The patients were suffering from a range of mental illness - some were labelled accordingly. One male patient had a disfigured face on one side; it was unpleasant to look at since the disfigurement seemed to be caused by sores. This man spent most of his time alone – it was unpleasant to sit next to him at mealtimes.

The atmosphere in the ward was gloomy. It was shabby and the wallpaper was dull, as was the furniture. It was easy to see that little money was spent on the environment. Again, a point that springs to mind is the importance of the hospital environment in the rehabilitation of mental illness. Why, I ask, is there still a poorhouse attitude to mentally affected patients? One day someone will come along and challenge the system...

Several weeks passed and I was given permission to leave the hospital at weekends. I was unable to go home, so I stayed with friends. The depression remained, so I was not much in the way of company. The misery increased at the end of the weekend, when it was time to return. The prospect of being in a dreary hospital for a considerable time to come filled me with horror. Weeks passed and there was no sign of improvement in my state. I had become friendly with two of the patients, both alcoholics, with whom I could muster some conversation.

I tired of woodwork and switched to typing classes instead. Again, there was little incentive to learn, as instructions are very limited. I forced myself to attend each day - I knew I had to try to do something. However, I was finding it hard to lift my spirits, even in the company of the few friends I had made.

After a couple of months at Springfield, it was eventually decided to give me Electro Convulsion Therapy, or ECT. I believed this treatment was applied with very bad cases of depression. I had received a short ECT treatment course many years ago and it had seemed to work then. However, I would have greeted the blow of a sledgehammer, if I had thought it would cure me.

The ECT treatment continued for some time - I cannot remember the number of sessions I had, yet unlike before, improvement did not result. That was a complete letdown; it was always in my head that ECT would cure me again. Whilst I was having the treatment, other patients were dreading the prospect of it. It was somewhat morbid prior to getting the treatment - the patients were lined up, waiting their turn. It was like queuing for the electric chair. I tried to console some of them by telling them it would not be as bad as they feared, but they were so frightened, I could not reassure them. The after effects of ECT are difficult to bear - the shock treatment leaves the patient with the mother of all headaches, but I thought this would be a small price to pay if it was successful.

Then, during the course of one of my treatment sessions, something went wrong, the cause of which the doctors could not determine. I was of course oblivious to this, and some time later the sister in charge told me that the doctors had been extremely worried about me and the cause and effect. I lay semi-conscious for over two weeks, not knowing what I was doing and apparently talking gibberish. I wandered out of the hospital grounds and could not be found.

One evening, I arrived back with a gash over one eye, which required eight stitches. Eamon Coyne, my good friend, came to see me in the evenings after work and would spend time looking after my needs. Other friends were also coming to see me regularly, even though I could not converse with them in a normal fashion. I think they were not sure of my condition. Was the way I was behaving a manifestation of my sickness, was I was semi-conscious, or was I going to be like this permanently?

Once again, I received no information from the medical staff as to what had gone wrong - surely an explanation was owed to me. Distance was maintained on all treatment levels - in all the time I spent at Springfield I rarely met my consulting psychiatrist.

When, after a few weeks, I regained consciousness, my memory was a complete blank; that period, post-ECT treatment, was lost to me.

I have often wondered since why it was never disclosed to me what had gone wrong, nor to my next of kin, my uncle Michael Farley. Apparently, I had behaved very badly. The night sister told me I had chased a young nurse around the ward, although she may have been teasing me. There were no further repercussions, and this outweighed any other worries that might have prevailed. The medical staff had wanted me to benefit from the ECT treatment and perhaps they did, in the end, learn from the experience. Maybe I detected a tiny improvement in the level of my depression, but not enough.

Time was moving on and it was approaching Christmas; a period that can make one feel even more depressed. The hospital buildings looked even drearier and did not help. The other patients who shared my condition did not seem to be improving either. Some were being transferred to other hospitals and some were returning to their homes. One chap was being sent to an alcoholic rehabilitation centre.

There were days when I did not feel too bad. Prior to being hospitalised, I had given up smoking, but inside cigarettes became a refuge again. I was told that to give up smoking soon after my operation would not be good, as the abstinence could lead to depression. Whilst you cannot hide behind a cigarette, for a mood swinger it does offer a certain comfort. A few of us used to regularly have a cup of tea and a smoke at around 5am - it was a thoroughly enjoyable ritual. The place was peaceful and gentle conversation would take place. This early morning social event lasted a couple of months - it was the only time I was ever at ease with myself at Springfield.

Nowadays, I wonder how at times I managed without smoking. At that time it was a consolation -

each draw on the cigarette brought comfort. Wherever there was a gathering of mood swingers there would be full ashtrays. Perhaps I am biased when, now, the emphasis is so much on not smoking. A little consideration should be given to what it offers to people who are mentally affected.

The days dragged at Springfield and as winter set in the grounds became strange. Although I was able to leave at the weekends, I was always down in the dumps. My friends took me for drives to different places, but even these diversions could not revive me. They made me feel even worse. Yet my friends continued to be kind, never voicing their worry or fear, and when it was time for me to return to the hospital it reminded me of schooldays, returning after the holidays, and how miserable I had felt.

I had been at Springfield since August - soon it would be Christmas and it looked like I would be there in the New Year of 1974. I had a few good short spells but there was still a lot of treacle in the works. I had never been this depressed for so long and it was beyond my power to make the short good spells have a longer duration. No matter what people do for me at these times, I cannot raise myself above this and then there is the feeling of guilt that I am letting everyone down. Christmas had always been a lonely time for me, so as usual I could not expect any improvement to take place during the season. I could not raise any enthusiasm for the New Year either - I had never understood the point behind its associated revelry. As I returned to the hospital I continued with my therapy, which was my typing. It was boring as I was not making much headway and no instructions were being given to me but I struggled on with it - at least I was occupying my mind.

Days passed slowly punctuated by intermittent patient fracas and somehow I felt less fearful and more settled. I had been nurturing a relationship with the day sister whose presence had a good influence upon me. She seemed to take a genuine interest in the patients and one could talk with her normally and rationally - my conversations with her actually engaged me. My depression remained as bad as ever and I continued to visit friends at the weekends. I felt bad that despite their help it could not lift me. There appeared to be no way out of my misery, however my conversations with the day sister continued and she became a very good friend within Springfield.

In April 1974 it was decided that I should be released. I certainly did not think I was ready for return to the outside world as I felt no better that when I had arrived. The prospect of facing the real world left me feeling that I had lead in my brain and in my boots. Once more, friends were on hand to help and I was able to stay with them rather than returning to my flat alone. I led a quiet social life and was not in any state to move around in company. My friends understood this. How wonderful they were to me. In a way they saved my life with their terrific support and understanding of my plight. Eventually I was able to go out to the pub occasionally to enjoy a couple of pints - as I was not being prescribed medication at the time it was okay to have a drink - however, I was not enjoying it as I would have done before. The depression was eating away inside of me - nine months is a long time to be hospitalised - one month out and I still felt much the same.

10. The Handicapped Life

In order to explain the meaning of this notion I will go forward in time in 1973 when I discovered about my mood swings. I will use the term manic-depressive instead of mood swings to help this explanation. I think it terribly misleading to use the word manic as it conjures up thoughts of madness and chaos. In short, it's a swing in moods from a high to a low or vice versa (bi-polar).

Now, everyone gets a high sometimes - 'normal' people we would say have moods of elation. Consequently, a low for 'normal' people is that of a feeling of slight depression. The major difference in a person suffering from manic depression is that he or she goes beyond a demarcation line of high and low as experienced by a 'normal' person. When a manic-depressive is low, he or she is a danger to himself or herself, in so far as they become suicidal.

Reaching the other side of that demarcation line can be likened to digging a huge black hole into which you sink and from which you cannot get out. Manic depressives lose all confidence in them self; sometimes they lose interested in their appearance and their very lives. They do not eat properly, and above all they want to stay in bed lying there like a vegetable, hoping that they may never awake again. The length of time of this low state of mind can vary between days and years. Please forgive me if I here repeat myself but it is such a difficult state to describe.

A high state can be very trying for other people, especially one's partner or carer. Here again there is a variation as to how high a person can swing, i.e. beyond that demarcation line. The affected person feels great, just like a king in his castle. He or she can appear arrogant and indeed, think that he or she knows all there is to know. Credit card spending can be one disastrous outcome of such a mood - credit for hundreds and thousands of pounds can be run up in the course of a day, and to make matters worse, the most ridiculous unwanted items are bought. In this respect I am lucky and I am not affected to strongly in this manner when I am on a high. Although I have noticed myself spending money freely when shopping or buying generous rounds of drinks in the pub, I have never bankrupted myself. I also would give money to charity or those who are down and out, heedlessly too...

This is not self-flattery, but how you feel when you are high. I remember a nurse in West Middlesex Hospital telling me that I might sell my house and give away all of money when in this state. I mentioned this to Eamon Coyne, my good friend, as I did not understand what she had meant, as I had no understanding or knowledge of my mood swings. Eamon replied jokingly, 'that's a laugh - we cannot get you to buy a second round of drinks in the pub!' The trouble is that in some instances when high, a person may, for example, buy six dining room tables which the store or shop will then refuse to take back, leaving one with a huge debt and a collection of unwanted furniture. Some married couples have an arrangement that respects this lack of control; the affected partner allows the other to possess all the credit cards and all written cheques require both signatures to be valid.

Once I went out into my garden and mowed the lawn at 3 am one summer morning; I did not think it abnormal and never considered how the neighbours would react. On another occasion, I can recall clearing away leaves at the front of the house, and not satisfied with clearing my own front porch cleared others as well. This took place at 4am and I sang happily (and loudly) as I worked, oblivious of any person or thing. Mood swingers are likely to go around talking to complete strangers. Undoubtedly, taken aback, the recipient responds by thinking 'we have a right twit here'.

This has a more pronounced effect for me as being Irish I am pretty outgoing and it is part of our culture to talk freely as we move around. People in the south east of England, by comparison, are reserved and so if you see me being chased down a high street by a woman with an umbrella, you will know what has happened. As for the telephone - mood swingers are forever using them; the trouble is that they could be on a call to Australia and treat it as a local call.

11. Other Health Complications

One March morning in 1973 I awoke with a terrible fright - it seemed as if I was experiencing a massive internal collapse. I hadn't a clue as to what was happening and was very scared. I attempted to go out to buy a newspaper and it took me three hours to walk 300 yards. I spent the whole day alone without calling anyone - how I did this I shall never know as I was suffering an agony of worry and unknowing.

Finally I rang Eamon, who took me to the casualty department of my local hospital. Upon examination it was discovered that I had had a thrombosis due to my haemorrhoids. This meant hospitalisation and eventually an operation, however, an immediate operation was out of the question due to my swollen physical state. I lay flat on my tummy with a napkin tied around me. The consultant came to see me every morning and instructed the nurses how to apply the napkin. Then he would settle it himself, stand back and hit my backside. I felt I would bang through the wall. I wanted to tell him he could take my place the next day and I would do the hitting!

Two weeks elapsed; the service staff went on strike, which resulted in emergency patients being kept under the hospital's care. I was sent home to nurse myself with the help of my friends. At that time I was living in Chiswick, and knew some girls that worked locally. During their lunch break they would come to visit me and we would share the time together over a few pints of Guinness. It was good for my condition medicinally and taken under my GP's agreement, although in moderation due to the drugs being prescribing to alleviate the pain. My GP told me how nasty a haemorrhoid operation could be - he had had one himself.

I had a nice break during the day and then the boys would come around at night and take me out. Two weeks passed and I decided that I could resume work on a part-time basis. In order to avoid the rush hour, I went into work at 6am and came home at 2pm as I felt fragile and needed to take care. I would then adjourn to the hostelry for my medicinal draught.

One lunchtime I rang Clive, the husband of Jenny, a friend of my former girlfriend, June. He seemed delighted to hear from me and when he found out I was unwell seemed very concerned. He asked where I was and I replied 'The Crown and Anchor'. In former years we had both frequented this pub so he knew it well. He never made it there and I decided that I would once again not learn what had happened between June and myself. Luckily I was in a good state of mind, or so I thought; looking back at this particular time, I could see that I was high.

In 1979 I began to experience pain with the discs in my back and I could not get an early appointment to see a consultant through the National Health Service. I mentioned to my doctor the possibility of having osteopathic treatment and he told me I could do this in the interim period, which in fact turned out to be twelve months. I had a few treatments with a cranial osteopath and my back seemed to improve. I was surprised to learn how the backbone connects to the brain, and therefore can cause depression. The osteopath was very knowledgeable in this area, and I attended him periodically, as need demanded. Life remained stable and as the year progressed nothing much of note happened. The monotony of the security job was becoming demoralising. An MP with similarly unsocial hours might be compared; however, his salary would be somewhat different and gainsay the sacrifice!

In April 1989 I got another health problem - pains in my arms and legs and swelling in these limbs. I received some medication from the doctor and he carried out some blood tests. I had to take time off work, and one week later when the results of blood tests arrived, the doctor thought that the diagnosis was gout, but was unsure. He made an appointment with the consultant in the hospital but I had to wait to see him. The pain worsened and so I went back to see my doctor a few weeks later. I told him how uncomfortable I felt and asked if I could see the consultant privately. He gave me a few hospital addresses and told me that I could try to make arrangements by myself. I telephoned a couple of them but there seemed to be an impediment with each - it was frustrating and in the end I had no luck.

Eventually, Arthritis was diagnosed and I got an appointment at the rheumatology department in the hospital and thereafter attended at three monthly intervals. I used to undergo a change of consultant every three months and I found this beneficial as it provided a difference of opinion in the treatment prescribed. For example, around this time one doctor suggested flexible splints for my arms and hands. I requested these from the physiotherapy department and they told me to return in a couple of days when they would be ready. I collected the splints and when I used them to operate the computer they were an excellent aid, indeed they became invaluable. It was funny wearing them around the house - if someone came to the front door, as I answered it there was a look of astonishment on their faces. Then it would dawn on me that not only was I wearing the splints, but also an orthopaedic collar around my neck. I must have looked like an escaped torture victim!

I expect that many people had expectations of 1994, and I was no exception. The start of the year passed and I was doing the usual things - visiting the doctors and going to the Fellowship meetings. About the second week of July I was not feeling well - a little dizziness, a peculiar sensation that overcame me, but no pain. I made an appointment with my GP, but I was not too concerned.

A couple of days later I had been due to take a neighbour shopping. I had told him I would be half an hour late that day, as I would have to have a lie down, as I did not feel well. I had the rest and my neighbour called. We were about to leave, and suddenly I collapsed. I remember shouting to my neighbour to call an ambulance. Then I blacked out and I do not remember anything further until waking up in hospital some time later. I was confused as to what had happened and what was happening.

What had actually happened was that I had been taken to West Middlesex Hospital, but they did not have a bed space for me. I was moved to St Thomas's Hospital, where I was in Intensive Care for over two weeks. I had suffered a major heart attack, and was very poorly for some time. From what I could gather, my family had called from Ireland, however, for some days the hospital could not give them a definite answer. My family and friends commented upon the comforting manner of the hospital staff.

I must have been out of intensive care for a short time when some of my relations visited me. My sister had come over from Ireland and was with them. I was still in a confused state and found it difficult to make conversation with them. When they left I found that I could not move around very much. The nurses had to come and lift me in and out of bed. It occurred to me as I lay there thinking that it was good that I had a physical complaint and that this has not been caused by mood swings. Even though my mood swings complaint was more devastating as far as I was concerned, to others it was something not discussed. All who were now coming to visit me had never come when I had made suicide attempts although I had been as close to death on those occasions as I was now. I think it is sad that after a suicide attempt one experiences so many feelings of guilt. I long for them to leave me and have no control over them.

107

I was well cared for by the nurses and doctors in St Thomas's. It took me a while to get used to feeling so very weak. Sometimes something happens unexpectedly and one is very touched by it. This recollection arises because I happened to mention to someone in the ward that the Test Match was being broadcast on television. A nurse overheard me and went and got a television for me to watch the cricket. She then went to great trouble to arrange it so that I could view it from my bed.

Unfortunately, I did not sleep whilst in St Thomas's. Different sleeping pills were prescribed without success. It puzzled me as to whether it was my heart condition or a symptom of my mood swings that was causing this sleeplessness. Not being able to sleep triggered of a bout of mania (a high). I did not want to cause a fuss, so decided to cope as best as I could.

I had been in St Thomas's for two weeks when I was taken back to the West Middlesex Hospital. I still had to be carried, as I was in a very fragile condition. I was not necessarily enjoying it, but, as I mentioned before, I was relieved it was a physical condition. I kept on analysing my situation: Now I was physically immobile whereas with manic depression I had been mentally immobile. Being mentally immobile had led to physically immobility, i.e. not able to move outside the house when depressed.

In the West Middlesex Hospital I received wonderful care. A special mattress was put in my bed to eradicate the discomfort, as I had been confined to bed for so long. A male nurse who was on the ward was extremely good to me. He had undergone a year of psychiatric training. I told him that I was a mood swinger; my good friend Denis Treacy had also told him. I was still not sleeping very much, and this was very frustrating. If I did close my eyes for a few minutes I was hallucinating. I found out later that it was due to all the drugs that were being pumped into me. My arthritis was causing me a great deal of pain and distress also.

Two weeks had passed and I was still very weak, still having to be lifted in and out of bed. Around this time I began to notice that I was going high. I mentioned this to the male nurse, but he thought I was OK. Some time later he came to check on me and after a while he agreed with me. He carried out a Lithium test, which took the form of a blood test and would determine if my Lithium levels were high or low. He found the level to be very low, and he phoned the psychiatric unit and informed them. The doctor who was attending the ward on a daily basis asked me if I could hold out with the mood swings until they stabilised my heart condition. I mentioned to him that the stresses of the mood swings were probably affecting my heart. He decided to leave things as they were for a couple of days. It took a whole week for someone from the psychiatric department to come and see me. To add insult to injury, it was just a trainee doctor who was sent.

He gave me Haloperidol and Diazepam to try to settle me down. I found after a couple of days that my mouth was dribbling; I had twitching in my face and could not maintain my balance. I telephoned a friend, Alan Mitchell, a member of the Fellowship, and described my condition. He said it was a reaction to the Haloperidol and that it took the form of pseudo Parkinson's disease. I thought to myself - great - I came in here with one illness and now I have three. I haven't asked for any seconds or thirds - thank you very much. It seemed like endless bad luck. The male nurse stopped the Haloperidol and Diazepam. I had not known until then that a patient has the right to refuse any drugs prescribed for him or her. The first couple of days after I got up it were like learning to walk all over again.

I was transferred from the Cardiac Unit to another ward. As I was by then able to walk a little this broke the monotony of not being able to sleep. One night a nurse spoke to me; I thought she was going to lecture me for wandering around. Instead, what a lovely surprise I got: she told me that there was a container of cooled milk around the corner and I was to help myself to a couple of glasses each night whilst I was there. Oh boy was that cool drink such a treat at about 3 am. I must have looked a sight, wobbling about as the pseudo-Parkinson's Disease was making me unsteady. I was controlling my mood swings quite well under the circumstances - at least there seemed to be no repercussions except for one exception - a young nurse reprimanded me for shouting on the telephone. Someone may have explained to her about my condition, as she later came and apologised to me.

One day I was a bit uptight, and was asked to get into my bed and to take things easy. A doctor was sent for and when she arrived she examined me and showed concern about my condition. She arranged for a second doctor to assess me. In the meantime I seemed to calm down a little. The doctor waited for a little while until she was satisfied that I was OK. She advised me to rest for an hour. I never did get to find out what was wrong. It must have been due to being so high - I became very stressed. This may have caused some trouble to my weak heart. I was still dribbling from the mouth, and experiencing tremors in my body caused by the Haloperidol.

I received one more visit from the psychiatric department and I told the doctor about the side effects of the medication I had been prescribed. We chatted for a while and nothing else was suggested. The remarkable outcome, which worried me, was that he did not mention when he would see me again in hospital. If this was not feasible, then it was imperative that a follow-up outpatient appointment should be made. I had one of my regular appointments about two months on from that time and it was ridiculous that I would have to wait so long for my psychiatric condition to be monitored again. In the event, that was exactly what happened, and I remain disgusted to this day that the system did allow it to happen. I saw my heart consultant within a couple of days. I told him I was keen to leave hospital as soon as possible. He examined me and said that I could return home provided I had a home help and meals on wheels, and took life very easy. I could leave in a week's time providing these arrangements were in place.

It was not out of lack of thanks to the hospital generally for the care they had given me that I wished to leave. My reason for wanting to leave was singular - I had sleeping tablets at home that worked for me. I could not obtain these tablets in the hospital. I had now been in hospital approximately six weeks, and that had meant six weeks without sleep. I was looking forward to some sleep at last. A person needs to experience a couple of nights without rest to experience the frustration it brings.

Due to all my ailments and afflictions I was a lot more disorientated than I allowed for at the time. Being high, I had to keep a tight rein on what I was doing. As I have explained before, when high, I would want to be doing several things at once. I got an early release from hospital after the home care arrangements were in place. An illustration of my frailty occurred when I climbed a ladder, a set of steps, to straighten a picture. I fell backwards onto the floor - it was a miracle I did not injure myself. Luckily, a friend who had a key to my front door, called by just as this was happening.

When I came around after the shock I gave myself, he told me in no uncertain terms how stupid my action had been. To add insult to injury, I received a letter from the Open University stating that I had failed the exam (part of my Masters Degree) that I had taken in

May. I would have to re-sit it a year later. Perhaps because of everything else that was happening to me I was not quite as disappointed as I might have been.

One week out of hospital, and I was able to venture outside the house, walking very slowly. Unfortunately the pseudo-Parkinson's Disease was adding to the weakness in my heart and making it difficult for me to get around I could not believe the extent of my immobility. Walking just as if I were drunk, I was all over the place. Any hill was completely out of the question and I could not attempt it.

Some days passed, and, thank goodness, I began to improve. One of my friends was able to take me out to the pub for lunch. I relished that meal, as the food provided by meals on wheels was awful. I had two half pints with my lunch. I could not lift the glass to my hands without tremors upsetting it. I remember my friend would pick up the bits and pieces, which I had been scattering around in the throes of trying to manipulate my fork and knife. My friend did all this discreetly, so as not to embarrass me. That friend, Denis Treacy, has been so good and understanding to me. Looking back, I think that without his support I would not have survived so well.

After two weeks of being out of hospital, my niece and her boyfriend arrived from Ireland to see me. Whilst they were here, my niece suggested that I should go to Ireland to convalesce. I preferred the idea of going to Eastbourne or Sussex, but upon the recommendation of family and friends, I decided that Ireland would perhaps be best. My niece booked the return flight for a two-month stay. She had trained as a nurse and gave me all the advice and help that she could. She returned to Ireland with her boyfriend after a week's stay. Three weeks later I set out for Ireland on what was to be the most ill fated trip of my life. Dennis Treacy took it upon himself to look after my house and car whilst I was away. He took me to the airport, and I was lucky that he was with me. I was still very fragile and in a crowded place, needed support.

I had visited my GP and he gave me a Nitro spray to put under my tongue when I suffered angina attacks. This replaced the tablets I was putting under my tongue and was more effective. I also went to the hospital for an appointment in the heart unit. My condition was found to be satisfactory, and I was prescribed other medication. My arthritis had been getting worse and I asked my doctor if I could be prescribed Cortisone to help the pain. He gave me some to be taken orally though I would have preferred an injection. A few days later the pain was even worse and got to be so bad that I went to the casualty department at the West Middlesex Hospital at 3am one morning. The doctor discovered that I had sciatica, and to make matters worse, I had shingles as well, but he would only give me a prescription for the shingles and gave me a letter for my GP, where responsibility lay, in his opinion, for the treatment of the sciatica.

I thought 'why me?' -life was being very unfair, especially after the recent traumas I had undergone. I went to see my GP and he prescribed medication, which made no improvement. Other medication was tried but to no avail. I was spreading chamomile lotion on my shingles, but after a month discovered it was having a detrimental effect. A fortnight after seeing the doctor who had introduced me to Tramadol tablet, I found that these were effective painkillers and also helped my arthritis. I thought the pain from the arthritis was bad, but the pain from the sciatica was much worse. The shingles were irritable and frankly very frustrating. I was now taking about twenty tablets a day. It was a full time job attending to my medication.

In October I went for my regular appointment at the psychiatric unit. This was the first time I had been seen since being in hospital last July and August when I had suffered the heart attack. I was very disappointed at not being seen straight away after leaving hospital. On that visit both the psychiatrist and myself agreed that I was going through a very up and down period. The psychiatrist arranged an appointment to take place in two months time. I also attended the rheumatology department - nothing new could be done for me. My health problems continued into the New Year. The sciatica and shingles lingered on for some time, but at least the painkillers eased the pain from the sciatica. I also obtained a Tens Machine, which gave some relief. The machine sends an electric current through two electrodes placed on the area in which one feels the most pain. I found it to be very soothing.

My condition remained the same until after Christmas. In early January 1995 the sciatica and shingles at last began to improve. I began to study for the re-sit of my exam that would take place in May. The studying helped to take my mind off my aches and pains. It puzzled me that I come through such a long bad period yet my mood swings were not yet seriously affected. It must have been God and some prayers that had saved me from a worse fate. It is also true that as my knowledge grew about mood swings, this helped me to cope with them better.

I continued attending my hospital appointments, psychiatry every two months and rheumatology every three months. Here I must give credit to the psychiatrist, he was now seeing me every two months and offered to see me at shorter intervals if I thought my condition worsened.

My angina was better now; I experienced occasional difficulty due to my heart condition, but with a whiff of the Nitro spray this disappeared. I continued to attend the rheumatology department and psychiatric unit regularly.

It was now May. I decided to put my house on the market. I had been thinking of doing so since I had had the heart attack. A ground floor flat would be much more suitable for my heart condition and me. I had discussed it with my doctor and with a few friends, to reassure myself that I was not doing anything silly. I recalled what the nurse had said to me a long time ago - I might want to sell my house when manic. I was not under any pressure to sell therefore time was on my side. When I did move I would try to stay in the same area, as I did not want a totally new environment affecting my mental state.

It was now 1997, and I was waiting for the signing of the contracts for the house. Eventually this happened and I moved into my new flat. A great trauma is often associated with moving house, but this was not the case with me. I had some wonderful friends to help me move. It is sometimes difficult to express thanks to them in the way I would like to. Because of the mood swings, ordinary people misread or cannot understand the true meanings I express. Mood swingers need more love affection and reassurance than most because of the character changes that mood swings bring about. I am a very sensitive person and am sensitive towards others. Sometimes I feel I have an enhanced insight into their character.

The ground floor flat eliminated the use of stairs, beneficial to my heart condition and mobility generally. I had not realised that because I have arthritis in most joints, moving up and downstairs had been as painful as getting up - coming downstairs is equally as difficult as going up, as the weight of the body is on one foot at a time. The flat was compact and much brighter than my former home.

I had been taking sleeping tablets since coming out of hospital nearly three years ago. In that time I had changed tablets about four times. They seemed to change their efficacy about every few months. I mention this in case someone else finds that one kind does not work. At about this time I was able to tell when to wean myself off them and was very pleased that I succeeded in this. I do wake up during the night and this is due to the pain I suffer from the arthritis. Once I get up out of bed and have a walk around for a spell I can then get back to sleep. Although sleeplessness is a symptom of mania I can discount that in these instances. For me not being able to sleep is frustrating and soul destroying. People who can sleep do not realise the agony and misery lack of it causes.

12. Treatments and Therapy

It was 1971 and I was experiencing a massive low. Early one morning I decided to go to Springfield Hospital to see my ward day nurse who had become such a good friend. It was an eight-mile drive across London, which was difficult given my sudden loss of confidence, but I hoped seeing her would revive my sense of self. I visited her several mornings before going to work; I was a little better for a few days but then began to feel down again. My doctor gained me admittance to hospital for observation, and doctors, social workers and therapists interviewed me. (I am assuming these designations, as I was not informed of them myself). It was decided that I should attend as a day patient and did so for two weeks. The therapy helped, I got better and returned to work. My colleagues were accommodating - in fact, nothing was said - it was offered as an excuse that I had needed a rest.

I was prescribed a drug called Lithium, in conjunction with other medication. In fact, I will explain the incident that revealed to me the beneficial effect it had on my mood swings. Sadly, this was twenty years after it was first prescribed to me, without any explanation of its importance and relevance to controlling my condition. That knowledge came to me in 1995 when I had a heart attack, and coming off Lithium acted as a detonator device.

When I was in Dublin in 1976, I had been alcohol free for twelve months and had been taking Lithium regularly. Whilst there, I began to drink socially and decided to stop taking the Lithium as I thought the combination of the two would be a bad mix. This triggered off massive highs, with alcohol exacerbating the problem, especially when consumed in large quantities.

In 1995, after I suffered my heart attack, the medical staff at the West Middlesex Hospital decided that the combination of Lithium, the drugs I was taking to control my arthritis and the drugs I was being prescribed because of my heart attack was dangerous. Without Lithium I went high, but at this time was more aware of the cause and effect. It was six months after my heart attack that I was able to draw this analogy between the two instances - coming off Lithium, on both occasions, had caused me to go high. I felt an immediate sense of satisfaction and relief as I had solved a mystery that had bothered me throughout the years. The combination of Lithium, the facility of being able to visit a psychiatric unit every three months, and the knowledge of the effect it had upon me served me well and enabled me to maintain a healthy balance. I was to take Lithium from now on.

I became cautious in my attitude towards parties and drinking alcohol, as I did not want to interfere with the Lithium balance. Christmas was approaching, always a depressing time for me, but contrary to my anticipation, Christmas passed amiably. I often try to analyse my mood swings: do events, or does time cause them? Alternatively, is it the chemical imbalance in the brain, so stated by the medical profession? Could it be a combination of both?

I have a simply analogy of a car battery. If the negative wire drops off, one becomes low. If the positive wire drops off, one becomes high. Then upon recovery, Lithium lifts the wires back on to the battery. The mood swings are then back to a *status quo.*

It was to my advantage that I had a change of doctors every three months. Through this, a cross section of opinion was given and I enjoyed the rapport I developed with each of them. The interesting characteristic that emerged was that the female consultants were by far the most sympathetic. It was now 1980 and five years since my last hospitalisation. I thanked God for his care, and for the last treatment I received - it had given me a marker for my good health. Months passed and I seemed 'normal'. I remain sceptical of this word, as society frowns on anyone who has had mental illness.

It was in 1981 when I had first learned that the doctors I was seeing in the psychiatric unit were training to become GP's. I had thought that I was seeing trainee consultant psychiatrists, and when I discovered this, I asked to see a consultant psychiatrist. No matter how hard I tried, I could not be accommodated. I could not understand how someone with my mental health record would not be seen at least a couple of times a year by such a professional. I made a number of requests, all to no avail.

Around this time, I wrote to the psychiatric unit that I would like an appointment to see the consultant psychiatrist. I made it clear in my letter that I was in no way being derogatory to anyone else that I had seen there. The next day, I received a telephone call from the hospital and from a doctor I had previously seen. He asked me to go along and see him: he wanted to know why I had written the letter. I replied that it was self-explanatory and that I was requesting to see his next in line. He was a highly-strung man and perhaps he thought he had done something wrong to me. He asked how I was and I responded affirmatively. He commented that he thought I was feeling a bit down, whereas I felt I was a little up if anything. Our conversation ended and the purpose of my letter received no further discussion.

Around September 1989 however, I began to experience tremors in my hands and legs. At one of the Fellowship meetings, one of the members advised me to see a consultant psychiatrist and I did just that. A few days later I went to the hospital and saw a psychiatrist. I recounted the recent health deterioration and she told me to wait and she would go and make

119

arrangements. A few minutes elapsed and she returned to confirm that I had an appointment the following day. I saw the consultant psychiatrist himself and he identified the problem - the Lithium I was taking to prevent mood swings was interacting with the medication I had been prescribed for arthritis. He reduced the Lithium dosage from 800mg to 600mg a day and said that that should alleviate the tremors.

It had taken me thirteen years to see this man and I felt cheated as every avenue I had taken had seemed to present a block. After all, if thirteen years earlier I had had contact with him; my life might have been different. During that period I might have been diagnosed as a mood swinger. All of my life, not just after I started work and commenced studying, I had been an advocate of information. Nowadays in commerce, it is regarded as our most important commodity. I think that the denial of information to me as a patient reflects badly on the health care system. Those like I, who are ill with mental affliction, deserve as good care and attention as if it were a physical affliction. I hope a political party will highlight this issue at some stage.

The change in the Lithium dosage did help the tremors, but I continued to suffer from them in a mild form. Unfortunately, they affected my studies and this was reflected in my assignment marks. I visited the hospital and they increased the level of medication for the arthritis. I was to go back for a consultation on a regular three monthly basis, at which time I would also see the consultant psychiatrist. Here my long association with trainee psychiatrists ended.

Although I was disappointed in not getting to see a consultant for such a long time, I must thank the trainees; some of them helped me a lot. On looking back, I can see that they acted as a kind of safety valve. As I saw them every three months, I could

120

unload my troubles to them - the fact that they were there for me was enough.

Around this time there was not much else to comment upon except that I could tell I was feeling down. The Rheumatology Consultant recommended that I should see an occupational therapist regarding the tremors in my hands. I was given a wax bath, which gave me a week's respite. Arthritis is a very painful illness and it is therefore very difficult to bear. All in all, I had to take fourteen tablets each day. I feel just like Moses - as the Lord said to him 'keep on taking the tablets!' It is OK when I take them at home because they form part of my daily routine. When I go away or on holiday the routine disintegrates and I end up having tablets everywhere. At home, I have my tablets in the appropriate room to correspond with the time that I have to take each one - it helps if the tablet is visible and available to remind me of the time I have to take it.

I had continued to do the exercises for my body and my fingers, and on my next visit to the hospital the doctor obtained an appointment for me for hydrotherapy. This consisted of doing exercises in a pool of lukewarm water under instruction from a therapist. I underwent six sessions of hydrotherapy and it helped the tremors considerably. The therapist also gave me instructions on exercises I could perform in a swimming pool, and I began to visit my local swimming baths twice a week to do the exercises gently. It helped to reduce the pain and the stiffness - both beneficial to everyday tasks. I began to go regularly to the swimming baths three times a week and increased the number of exercises I did each visit, but was careful not to over do them.

It was coming up to the summer of 1990 and I had seen my consultant psychiatrist a few times. He had seemed satisfied with my progress and mental state. He suggested changing my Lithium treatment to that of a drug call carbamazepine but then decided against doing so as the Lithium was working well and it was getting near the time when I would be attending Summer School for the 'Global Politics' course. I was not in the best of conditions to go, and my absence would have been excused, but the tuition I would receive would be invaluable, as I would have to sit two exams this year.

I continued to attend the psychiatric appointments every three months. Although not a lot was necessarily discussed at those meetings, they were helping me to remain a more stable person. The consultant always enquired as to how my studies were progressing, as he knew how therapeutic they were for me.

13. Gabrielle

In June 1980 I visited Scarborough and arranged to meet a friend, Joan, there. When we met I felt that she had aged in appearance. I had not seen her for about eighteen years, but felt that it was perhaps more than the passage of time that had been the cause of this. During our conversation, she mentioned that her daughter Gabrielle, who lived in America, was in a lot of trouble. She drank heavily and neglected herself; she had married and divorced twice. Her first husband had been very rich and they had seemed to be happy. However, even after the divorce was granted and they had separated, he would have wished to have Gabrielle back. Her second marriage was a disaster from the beginning. This husband was nearly twice her age and they rowed with each other constantly.

Gabrielle and I had grown up together and had been very close, virtually childhood sweethearts if you wish. There was a close bond between us, perhaps she also regarded me as the brother she had never had. Her grandmother had reared her as her father was an engineer and both parents lived abroad for long spells. Each year they came to Ireland and took a bungalow by the sea. I was always invited to join them and they felt like my second family. It was like a fairy tale to me as I was able to enjoy things that I would have otherwise never experienced. Staying in a bungalow by the sea was the privilege of the wealthy and whilst with them I enjoyed many luxuries.

On looking back, I think that Gabrielle was unhappy that she was separated from her parents for such long periods and these short holidays were not enough to compensate. That they left her short of nothing material did not replace the emotional family stability that she longed for as a daughter - I mention this now as it forms the framework for what was to follow.

I was very sad for Joan and Gabrielle when I heard the outcome of the recent years and felt very sad to leave Joan without being able to help. I could now understand why the last eighteen years had taken such a toll on her looks and appearance. After I returned to London I thought about Gabrielle a lot, but having not seen her for such a long time, there was a distance.

In 1991 The Social Club at Unigate was planning a trip to Florida in September, and I decided to go. I knew that Gabrielle lived there and I wondered if I should call her up during my stay. Was this interfering or was it renewal of old friendship? Would her family mind? Would I be drawing trouble to myself? I rang my sister and asked her advice. She felt it would be a good thing for me to do and that I should ring Joan and let her know before I left for the US. Joan in turn was delighted when I told her I was planning to see Gabrielle.

September came and on the evening before my departure, as I was preparing for my trip, I had a phone call from Joan. She told me that Gabrielle had been in a fire and has been badly injured and begged me to see her as soon as I could after arrival in Miami. I arrived late on Saturday night; on the Sunday a friend and I went to an early morning service at church. Gabrielle preoccupied me and I asked a young priest where the hospital was located. He replied that he did not know. As things turned out we both had our origins in the same county of Ireland. We asked members of the congregation for directions. They were most helpful as the hospital was well known; it was located at the other end of town and they warned us off a run-down area we would have to go through halfway through the journey. We had just one change of bus en route and it was far from that tricky spot.

We arrived at the hospital much more easily than we had anticipated and asked directions to the ward in which Gabrielle was being nursed. It was an intensive care ward and therefore I was not allowed to take the flowers I had brought for Gabrielle inside. The nurse gave me a cap and gown to wear in case of infections, and when I finally approached Gabrielle's bed I could see that she was covered from head to toe in bandages. The impression was that of a mummy. I spoke just a few words of greeting and she recognised my voice at once. I was amazed and delighted, as we had not seen each other for some eighteen years and now, under the disguise of the cap and gown, she certainly would not have recognized me.

Gabrielle was feeling sorry for herself, saying that there was no love in her life. She said there had been no love when she had been growing up, no home life, and that her relationship with her parents had been distant and of a love-hate nature. I responded by saying that such thinking would have no good effect upon her or her current predicament.

The nurse came to say it was time to go and that Gabrielle needed to rest again. I said that I would visit her the next day. When we were outside the nurse said to me, "I do not know who you are or where you came from, but that girl was dying and now has decided to live". She explained that the pain Gabrielle was suffering from her burns combined with the alcohol she had consumed had had an altered effect on her mind. As we walked down the corridor there was a noisy exchange and the nurse informed me that it came from Gabrielle's companion, a chap who was so abusive and inebriated he had been refused admission to see her several times.

I cried all the way back to the hotel: it was evident that Gabrielle was in a bad state both physically and mentally. It was going to take a huge effort on her part to get back to good health and well-being. I wrote to my Uncle Michael and explained, as explicitly as I could, what the situation presented. I also emphasised that a member of her family should come out to Miami to be with her. I asked my Uncle to convey what I had written to Gabrielle's family. I felt sure that they would respond to his diplomatic implorations better than mine.

The following day my friend and I went on a tour around Miami. In the afternoon when we approached the area in which the hospital was located I dropped in to see Gabrielle. She had no other visitors. Whilst I was there the telephone rang and she dropped it three or four times. Her hand had been badly burned and the bandaging made it difficult for her to grip anything. I observed that it was awkward for her to manage the shape of the telephone. She said that it was good therapy for her and she wanted to put up a good fight against her injuries. We reminisced for some time during that visit and all she could remember from times long gone given the mess she was currently in surprised me. She repeatedly implored me to 'stay another while', which I did.

When I left the hospital the last bus had gone. An old man told me not to linger near the bus stop as I was not safe and that I should return to the hospital and telephone for a cab. I went back and was looking for a telephone kiosk when a lady came up to me and asked what the matter was. I told her my story and it turned out that she was a doctor at the hospital and would be leaving in an hour and would drop me off at my hotel. Later she came back and said an emergency admission necessitated her to stay and recommended that I get a taxi to the nearest bus route I would since have a chance of catching.

I was scared out of my wits waiting - there were all kinds of reprobates hanging around. I got a taxi all the way to the hotel, but did not have sufficient cash to pay my fare. I then had to convince him that I would return. Luckily, my friend Mickey was staying in a hotel adjacent to mine and I was able to borrow the change needed to pay my fare. What a night - one I have never forgotten.

The following day I thought I would go early to see Gabrielle. When I arrived she was very poorly and suffering from exhaustion. She had just received treatment and this had taken a lot out of her. She murmured to me to come back later to which I replied, 'I have rushed all the way across Miami to see you and now you are telling me to go away.' That raised a small smile, as she understood my sense of humour. I went away, had a meal, wandered around the area, and returned to the hospital after a few hours had gone by.

By this time she was more alert and told me a lot about her adult life. She had been a model; her photographs had appeared in Vogue and other fashion magazines. She had done some acting and had shared a flat with Liza Minnelli at one time. She and a partner had opened a boutique on the Virgin Islands. She was not in anyway boastful of her varied and interested past life and life styles. She was dismissive of her marriages and commented that they had both been mistakes. She complained that when she had been a child there had been no love in her life and she had hated being at boarding school. In the circumstances I found her I could not help but feel sad for her. I hoped my company was helpful and bade her farewell, bearing in mind that I had to leave earlier than the previous evening in order to catch the bus.

The next day Mickey and I went to Fort Lauderdale and upon my return to Miami that evening I again visited Gabrielle. The next couple of days we spent sightseeing and I managed to get to see Gabrielle at the end of the day. She had no other visitors and so I tried to telephone her a few times during the day. The time of my holidays was ending and I told Gabrielle that I would write and that she must be very brave in the face of her misfortune to overcome it. Back in England I felt sad for her in the situation she was

127

facing. Each week I wrote to Gabrielle and I felt this to be an absolute duty, having experienced the seriousness of her state.

I had received a Valentine card from Gabrielle. Someone had written it for her and she had managed to scrawl her signature. Her hand injuries were still severe.

Then news arrived from Gabrielle that she was coming to England at the beginning of April to visit her family. I remained high and this state was not discerned by others or myself around me. When I met Gabrielle to take her to her family's home in Scarborough, much to my disappointment I could see that she had had a few drinks. Joan, her mother, was furious, having deduced the same. I drove them all to Scarborough and a reunion with her father.

It was an unpleasant evening. Joan found a bottle of Bacardi in Gabrielle's luggage, and this resulted in a row, which continued into the night. The next day I had to return to London and Gabrielle came with me, as she would not stay with her parents. Upon arriving in London, I arranged with my friend Patricia to collect Gabrielle in the morning from my home, and for me to collect her in the evening from Patricia's home. In this way, I knew that she would be cared for and watched over. In fact, Patricia and Gabrielle were to become good friends.

Patricia had a little boy of four years of age and Gabrielle and he got on well too. From the outset of this arrangement, I made clear the rules concerning alcohol consumption for Gabrielle. I would allow her a diminishing amount of Bacardi per day whilst she would make all efforts to try to end her dependency.

We met up with Gabrielle, her mother and a friend and I gave all three a tour of London sights. I visited the West Middlesex Hospital and enquired if Gabrielle's injuries could be treated there. They felt, yes they could treat them, however, it would be much better if the hospital currently treating her continued to do so. They would also treat the alcohol problem, but the physical treatment was the priority. I conveyed this information to Joan and told her that Gabrielle could be admitted and Joan could stay with me whilst this was happening. She gave little enthusiasm in her reaction to these proposals and so I thought I had done as much as I could. Gabrielle was in no state to make decisions on her own. She had a letter instructing her to go back to the hospital in Miami in July. She decided that she would see how things progressed in the interim months.

As for Gabrielle, she seemed to be on the mend until Patricia told me that six weeks on she had seen her buying a bottle of Bacardi. When she returned to my house that evening, I challenged her on this - I asked her where she was in her progress with the reduction programme? By this time she should have been down to a quarter bottle a day - a goal we had discussed and mutually agreed. Whilst apparently reducing her consumption, she had been secretly increasing. I told her there would be one final warning and then she would be made to leave. I suggested that she should visit her mother in Scarborough and she agreed to go along with her father who worked in London. She had arranged to stay with them for a week but she was back in London within two days.

It was now June, and Gabrielle was due to return to the US at the end of the month. She produced the letter from the hospital in Miami, which actually said it was imperative that she resumed her treatment there by July. She asked me what she should do; I replied that it was her decision and hers alone. I next heard her say that she had been happier staying with me in London than she had been for a long time and that maybe we should get married. I replied that once she had made a recovery from her injuries, attended a clinic to help her stop her drinking; there would be plenty of eligible men available to her.

At the end of the month she returned to Miami. I knew it was not the best place for her to be, but it was necessary for her to continue her treatment. Other than the hospital, Miami was the worst place for her to be. I recall I once spoke to a lady there and her summation of Miami was that it had been abandoned to sex, drugs and drink.

Gabrielle was contacting me periodically and complaining of her unhappiness. I knew she had a dramatic tendency, and so I appeased her as well as I could. I told her in December that I would come out to visit her in Miami early in the New Year and contacted her parents in Scarborough to arrange to see them also. They invited me to stay with them over the Christmas period if that would suit my plans.

I took off for Scarborough on Christmas Eve and was warmly welcomed by Gabrielle's parents. When I was a youngster, I had always regarded Joan as a good aunt, particularly during my childhood holidays, which I shared with them by the seaside. During the few days I stayed with them, our conversation centred on Gabrielle.

Like any parents, they were concerned about their daughter and her future life. They told me that her first marriage was to a wealthy businessman and that she walked out leaving her entire wardrobe and all her belongings. Her second marriage was to a chap much older than she was, and he had treated her badly. Eventually she ran away and met up with a fellow, again an older person. From their account, I gathered that her drinking problem had arisen some years ago and worsened as time went on. Joan had visited her in Miami a number of times, but her advice was always rejected. Joan had met her latest companion, Jim. Whilst she did not dislike him, she had little regard for him. I returned to London after a four-day stay.

I went to Miami without any knowledge of what the situation there would present. Gabrielle and Jim collected me from the airport, and I stayed in a hotel near where they lived in the suburbs. They were living in part of the house that remained intact, after it had mostly burned down. Gabrielle's friend Patricia was living in the neighbourhood and, from what I could surmise, Gabrielle was drinking heavily again.

My observations on Jim were that he had a Svengali flavour about him. I was told that prior to Gabrielle coming onto the scene he had had a young girl, a judge's daughter, staying with him. Patricia was able to give me some account of his history. He was divorced and his wife was a reformed alcoholic. Jim's family had a large contracting business, which he had inherited. Having been a heavy drinker himself for a time, the business had become neglected and dwindled. Luckily, he was now alcohol free and trying to keep alive what was left of the business.

I thought that everyone in Miami was an alcoholic from what I had seen so far. One day I was having a drink in the bar on my own. The waitress was telling me she had a daughter at school in Europe, and she hoped to keep her there. She said that in Miami now drink and sex were secondary only to drugs and that the city was not fit for any decent person to live in, at least as far as she was concerned. It was not long before I saw for myself her point and she might be right in her opinion. Jim's son, who worked in the business, arrived at the house one morning; his hand and shoulder were bleeding. His wife, who was on drugs, had attacked him with a knife. One of Jim's other sons was in jail for drug dealing.

Then one day, when I was out driving with Patricia, my suspicions surrounding Gabrielle's drinking were confirmed. She would not come with us on the drives we took so Patricia took me sightseeing. She wanted to show me as much as she could to return the favour I had given her when she visited England. She told me she had good reasons to believe Gabrielle was also taking drugs. She also said that Jim had a prostitute who visited him frequently and it was she who provided Gabrielle's drug supply.

On the up side, she told me that Gabrielle had been off alcohol for about three months after coming out of hospital, after her round of burn treatment had ended. She commented that it was a pity that her family did not come out to stay with her, and that if perhaps they had shown more care, things might have turned out differently. She also commented that Jim had been very good to Gabrielle when she came out of hospital. He dressed all her wounds himself for a long period of recuperation. He had great patience. Patricia also believed that Gabrielle had probably set his house alight whilst she was inebriated.

When I was once in the local bar, the young people there all seemed to be on drugs - they were slipping out the back door every now and then to smoke pot. I got talking to a very nice young girl who told me that she was a bank clerk. She told me she was on drugs - most young people were. I told her I was a friend of Gabrielle's, and she then mentioned when she had gone back to drinking, after coming out of hospital, the bar refused to serve her. She had looked so pitiful, covered in bandages and in such bad shape she was horribly pathetic to behold.

When her appearance improved and the bar began to serve her, the same girl told me that she had often escorted home, much the worse for drink. She also pointed out three prostitutes in the pub. I was amazed at the normality of their appearance. I had had a drink with one of them a few times; she was one of a couple that supplied drugs to Gabrielle. On another occasion, a young girl no more than sixteen years started talking to me. She thought I was Scottish and liked my accent. Whilst we conversed, she drank sixteen shots of whisky within an hour and a half. She walked away from me as though she had just sucked on a sherbet!

One weekend during my stay, a friend of Gabrielle's, Judy, invited us to visit a house she had on Palm Beach. It was a lovely drive and the house was in a nice location. Patricia was moving to the house shortly, and she wanted Gabrielle to share it with her. I thought this would present an ideal solution for Gabrielle and would extricate her from the mess that her life was currently in. Gabrielle resolutely refused and at the time I could not understand her utter rejection of the invitation. Later I realised why it was a totally unacceptable alternative to her - it would remove her from her drug supply and access to liquor. Judy was herself a reformed alcoholic - Gabrielle was fearful that she might attempt to reform her. One justifiable reason for her rejection was that Judy had a mother fixation about Gabrielle.

Miami was becoming another ball of string to unravel and, in all truth, whilst I could write a completely separate book about my visit there, it would be impossible for me to rationalise any of the goings on. Judy had two sons, whom we visited on the way back. They lived in two large ranch-like houses. I had the impression that there was great affluence in the family. I met another of Judy's sons during my trip, who could have taken me on his large cruiser for a sea trip were it not for business entertaining he was conducting on board. I had said to him that it was one of my greatest dreams to sail or crew a large sea-going yacht, although I was not sure that I would have been physically up to the demand of crewing.

I was very disappointed that his business commitments prevented my sea going experience. Sailing craft have always attracted me and I find that even looking at little dinghies is therapeutic. I had intended to be in Miami for three weeks but the airline I had travelled with, Freddie Laker, went bankrupt during my stay. There were no flights available and I had to curtail my holiday and return with another airline when the possibility presented itself. It was sad to leave so soon, as I felt I had needed all of that time to get through to Gabrielle. Now it felt as though the time spent there had been useless on that score, wasted. However, I felt that the trip had been worthwhile in spite of all its unexpected events.

Negotiation is often the result of a long series of consultations and talking - the more you talk the greater the chance of success. I was not going to have the luxury of time to achieve this success with Gabrielle, and I was being deprived of the last week in which I had intended to really focus on her present and future plans. When I set out on my mission, I had not known what it would entail and what unknowns would appear unexpectedly. Some people would not even have contemplated taking on the responsibility. I, however, felt optimistic about the influence I could affect her with. That, combined with the real care and concern I felt for Gabrielle and her parents, was a reality.

The evening before I left I gave her a lecture and told her in no uncertain terms where she was coming from and where she was heading. She had always boasted how much she loved her grandmother - I told her how disgusted her grandmother would have been with her current lifestyle and that she would have disowned her. This really hurt Gabrielle, as the love of her grandmother was a strong part of her self-esteem. I also tried to point out how many good things her parents had done for her. It was time for her to reciprocate and all she had to do was to act responsibly for her own life. I must have been extremely forceful as she burst out crying and ran away, obviously frightened by the tough truths I had said.

The following morning I was not in her favour. Before I left, I got her and Patricia together and told them that I had deposited £600 in a bank account for Gabrielle. I told her to get out of Miami and its cesspool and that the money was intended to enable her to do this. I felt doubtful that she would see things the way I did and I thought to myself 'she will never leave Miami, and she is too far down the road now'.

The time of being in Miami played hell with my mood swings and emotions - it had been a deadly cocktail to take and I was lucky that it did not rip me apart.

Letters were being exchanged between Gabrielle and me. I worried about her, but my hands were tied. She wanted that we should get married; I had told her if she could give up drinking and drugs we could think about it. I had previously told her if she got herself rehabilitated, fellows would be lining up to meet her. Then she could be so dramatic, I never knew what was really going on in her head. I was worried now that she was feeling rejected. At 3am on sleepless nights, I would turn it over in my head. When I am high, time does not matter. One night in this state I got out of bed and dressed myself.

I decided to go and see my parish priest as I thought it best to consult him. Having reached the house I rang the bell, after a few minutes the priest appeared. He probably thought - what have we got here? He did look bewildered, but in fairness he agreed to see me. I asked him if what I wished to say could take the form of 'Confession'. This is to say I was sincere in all my thoughts and deeds throughout my life, and especially in my dealings with Gabrielle. I now felt that I should tell her I would marry her. The priest sat there - I had a lot of baggage to recount - he was probably flabbergasted, and wondering to him self 'what am I doing sitting here listening to this Confession at this time of the morning?'

He was very considerate, said little and listened a lot. I did not expect any answers and I felt relieved at having someone who would just listen to me. Perhaps I was being devious, trying to get God on my side. It would have been fairer on the priest if he had known of my condition and mood swings, as he then would have understood the situation and my predicament.

Following the Confession, I decided I would write to Gabrielle and tell her I would marry her, but only under certain stipulations. I knew she sought security, but could not make up her mind between surrendering the drink and drugs in order to achieve this goal. Even though there was a great bond between us, I felt her attitude was that of 'when all fruit fails, welcome haws'. As I expected, I received an ecstatic letter back from her, in which she described how her grandmother would have loved this news if she had been alive.

I then called her bluff - I sent her a one-way ticket to London, together with some money to cover any incidental expenses she might have. It might be noticeable to a neutral observer that I had adopted a more cynical attitude and that in this admission of help, one can see it was doomed to failure. The response came and the excuse was that there was something wrong with her passport. This spelled out the wisdom of my thinking. We exchanged letters for about six months, which contained delicate hints from Gabrielle about money through her hard luck stories. The passport saga continued to be cited as an issue although she continued to talk about coming to England. Of course, having been an actress, she knew how to play her lines and I knew all along that her coming to England would never materialise. Then all communications ceased between us. This was the end of our relationship and whilst it might have made me feel foolish it didn't, mercifully. I had genuinely tried to help Gabrielle and it was not meant to be.

I may have been naive, but I was experienced enough now to see her strategies. Her not coming to England would save me a lot of strife. I would have had to deal with a lot of family politics, both hers and mine, and it would take a lot of patience to reform Gabrielle. Also what would I do if I suffered a relapse and could not handle my mood swings? I began to count my blessings and to see how the sending of the air ticket had been a masterstroke. It was a small price to pay to retain my peace of mind. I could now resolve my own domestic affairs and plan my future studies with the Open University. For me, the chapters dealing with Gabrielle's insoluble problems were closed. I would never have been able to rehabilitate her and it might have interfered with my own progress, a matter of relative importance to me.

Then, one day years later I had a real surprise, a telephone call from Gabrielle. She was in Scarborough for her sister's wedding. To my horror, I realised I had received an invitation, but had omitted to respond - there had been no mention of Gabrielle coming over for the occasion. I wondered if her parents had all along been afraid that I would be successful in persuading her to come to England and this was something they did not want. Now it was just a week before the wedding and too short notice for my employers to organise cover in my absence. I had to decline the invitation to join the family for their celebration. Gabrielle meanwhile had plans to visit London - she was now a reformed character and belonged to the AA - she looked forward to seeing me shortly after the wedding.

She arrived in London accompanied by her mother, and we went out altogether a few times. If we went for a drink she took something soft, but often made excuses to go to the toilet or make a telephone call. Such behaviour aroused my suspicion that the reform was not complete and that she was getting a drink from either another bar or disappearing to take drugs. However, I had a sense of relief in the knowledge that this was not my responsibility; I had made up my mind some time ago that it was an impossible situation. She gave me back the airline ticket (which she could not cash) and then told me that she and another girl were in the process of setting up a cleaning company and that a number of friends had invested in its establishment. Then came the question I had been expecting - would I make a contribution of £200 towards it? I told her I would consider the proposal and we arranged to meet again in a couple of days.

It was evident to me that this was a ploy to get more money from me. I felt an idiot in having given money to her before, and yet again to be taken for a ride. In order to reach a decision I asked some friends their advice - they thought I would be throwing good money after bad. I felt that if I did give her the money, it would be the last time I did so, and that that might hail the finalisation of our relationship. Finally I asked a priest, should I give her the money. He said 'if you feel happy to do so, go ahead.' Then he gave me a lecture in moral values, how she had divorced twice, and I left feeling that this had not been the point of the discussion. I decided to give her the money, even though it was a foolish action, and that this would be the last time I would bale her out. She was living in Miami, she would never reform, and when I met her the following evening I gave her the cash. She told me that she and her friend were determined to make a success of the venture as I drove her to the airport, and before leaving she was categorical about keeping in touch. I thought to myself 'yes and pigs might fly' as the plane took off - it was the end of my association with Gabrielle.

It was now 1994. In addition, I had heard nothing further from Gabrielle. This was not as I had expected although it may have been just as well, as she would surely have dragged me down. I did feel sorry for her and wondered if she had finally come to a bad end - how sad an outcome for someone who had so much talent.

Around July time, I was sitting at home when the telephone rang - it was Gabrielle calling from Miami. It had been three years since I had seen her, and by now I had succeeded in almost forgetting her existence. She asked if I could lend her some money as she had been injured in a car crash. I responded that money was scarce and that I was not having the best of times. I told her to call back the following evening and that I would give some thought as to whether I could help her or not.

It had been with great hesitation that I had given her money the last time she had requested it and I had vowed then that it would be for the last time. In truth, giving her money was inappropriate as she was truly beyond any real help that I could have given her when she mattered to me. This time, the answer had to be no and when she called back the following night I told her so. She had no apology for me concerning her lack of contact during the last few years and I made no reference to anything in the past. The conversation was short and to the point - I had no remorse - I had tried to help and now this was beyond me.

A few months later I received news that Gabrielle had died in America. Her mother rang me from Scarborough to say she had been hit by a car - this had been the cause of her death. I have other thoughts on this; she was at last out of Miami forever and how sad that she had wasted what could have been such a good life.

14. Ireland and Family

I had decided to visit my brother in Ireland. Everyone thought it a good idea. I would take the car, and I would not have to do much driving; I would be able to use it for relaxed journeys and to visit Kinsale, the picturesque town where my brother lived. One of my friends drove me to Ireland, as physically, my haemorrhoidal condition would not allow me to drive long distances.

I stayed with my brother and his wife, but this arrangement was soon to prove disastrous. My sister-in-law was having trouble with her car, and being a district nurse, was justifiably concerned. I, playing Sir Galahad, came to the rescue and offered her the use of mine. Then she asked me to accompany her on her patient calls, as she was not familiar with the way my car drove. Some of her patients were known to me, or knew of me, since my mother had been brought up in Kinsale. Then without any prior warning, my sister-in-law verbally attacked me and said I was interfering with her patients. I remembered the saying 'hell hath no fury like a woman's scorn' - boy was she mad.

I was in my brother's house for a short time when I began to detect 'vibes' coming from him and his wife - apparently they were jealous of me. It is only with hindsight that I now know I was high. Surprisingly, my sister in law, who claimed to know everything about medicine, did not see this either. There was a festival taking place in Kinsale and I was involved in its organisation. It was good fun - a diversion - and I knew many of the others involved; besides it was natural to have a few drinks around the planning of the festival's programme.

Maybe I was drinking too much, but I was in no way disorderly. Of course I did not know then that there was a correlation between mood swings and alcohol. As far as I was concerned, I was having a good time, and not stepping on anyone's toes. In the house I was subject to glares; I thought they could not understand how someone could be carefree and happy.

After two weeks the crunch came. The festival hosted a singing competition. The landlords of one of the pubs asked me to sing. I said I would. I had a friend in England who had once sung in a pub and when she wanted a rest she called me up to sing - I was no stranger to the stage. The night arrived and I had my little bit of fun, but my brother and his wife thought differently.

When I arrived for lunch the following day, my brother confronted me and said I was making a fool of myself around town and that I should pack my bags and go. I didn't utter a sound, but packed my bags. As I was loading my belongings into the car, he came outside and hauled me into the house, striking me on the chin. I dropped to the floor. I could not believe it; I had never been struck by anyone before. From that day to this I can still feel the hurt. My brother, seeing the wrong he had done, put his arms around me. For me it was too late - he should have been judging his own action and not mine, as had formerly been the case.

I was stunned, from not only the blow, but this incident was taking place in front of my brother's family. Considering his reputation as being that of a good family man, this behaviour was not commensurate. His morals surely should tell him no one has the right to act as judge, jury and executioner. To crown all of this, my brother then invited me to go with him for a drink, perhaps he thought this would redeem all or, at least, his violent gesture.

In order to appease him, I agreed, with some reservations. My only thought was now to get away as soon as possible as I no longer wanted to be subjected to their judgmental views. The pub we chose was televising the English Cup Final - it suited my mood, as

I was not inclined to talk. The more I drank, the more sober I became a contradiction in terms but nonetheless true. I guess no quantity of alcohol was going to eradicate the horrible experiences that the day had wrought.

We returned to the house having spent three to four hours in the pub. A quiet atmosphere existed there until bedtime. Sleep did not come easy for me that night and the morning could not arrive quickly enough for me to get away. Then I was driving at 70 mph - a lethal speed on those narrow roads, but the speed I was driving at did not enter my head once. At 6 am I was on my way, heading for my hometown, 25 miles away. I was oblivious of my driving - I wasn't concentrating at all - not thinking straight.

Luckily there was little traffic, in fact hardly any. I should reiterate here that I was still slightly high but could not recognise this. My main concern was to prevent myself from getting depressed. The meaning of highs and lows meant nothing to me at this stage and mood swings, (manic depression), were as yet not diagnosed or identified as a mental illness. When I mention highs I should explain that it is wholly in retrospect that I am able to recognise that state of mood. Depression - what I regarded as my long-term illness - was what I was always scared of.

When I arrived in my hometown I went to stay with some very good friends. Since the death of both of my parents, their place had been home for me whenever I went to Ireland. I spent around three weeks there and it certainly gave me solace and the opportunity to forget the incident that occurred in Kinsale. I was reporting to my head office every two weeks in order to keep them informed. Really, time did not seem to matter and I was enjoying myself - well that's how I felt.

My colleagues at work must have thought I was like a character from a James Bond movie - flying about the place.

I did return to Kinsale but ensured that I did not have any further contact with my brother. This time around I had a very nice and untarnished holiday. I returned to England much wiser about other people's attitude to me.

It was around May 1976 that I took the decision to go to Ireland with some friends from the Social Club at Unigate. We arrived in Ireland and went to our hotel where we had an evening meal. Afterwards most people retired to the bar - I was invited but declined - I had been abstinent for some months as a result of taking medication. The pub culture in Ireland is so much of a social tradition, it is almost impossible to avoid. You can happily enjoy the convivial atmosphere whilst sipping a soft drink, but whilst everyone around you enjoys a beer or a few measures, it becomes an irresistible allure.

Over the next few days I decided to suspend my medication, as I knew that I would want to share in a few drinks. We went on coach trips; invariably stopping at a number of places of interest and of course, had a few drinks at each. A week had passed and the tour was coming to an end. On the final evening a gala dinner and dance was to be held. I withstood the temptation to have more than just a few drinks, quite a feat as all were in a party mood.

My stay in Ireland lasted for another two weeks, as I wanted to see friends and family, and attend to some personal business matters. I hired a car in Dublin, decided to drive to Cork and onto my hometown. I stayed with very good friends of mine who were like family, Paddy and Kitty Houlihan. During the days, I drove to different places that I had not been to for quite a while. Some days I did very little driving, attending to personal business matters, seeing solicitors and visiting various administrative offices. For anyone not familiar with Ireland, I must describe how frustrating such experiences can be.

Everything in Ireland on an administrative level, twenty years ago, was done tomorrow, but that tomorrow never came. It was always achieved in the end, but accompanied by a lot of frustration and trepidation. Unfortunately, I had refrained from taking medication through most of the stay, which gave me license to drink, and offering no excuses for my own misdemeanours - I was drinking a lot at night.

As I said earlier, the pub culture is one you are expected to join in. However, I was taking in an abundance of brandy every night, and I was convincing myself that this was OK, as long I was not taking Lithium. During the days I did not drink as I was driving, (blissfully ignorant of how long alcohol remains in the bloodstream), visiting friends and sharing reminiscences of our youth. One remarkable reference that kept arising in many of our conversations was the value of the things that we had had, rather than not had, in our upbringing.

After a week my sleep pattern had begun to change - I would awake at 4am and then find it impossible to sleep again. I felt there was no point in lying in bed, got up and dressed and went to visit my friend, Dennis, at his place of work. He was a baker, and started work at 3am so I could go and have coffee and a chat with him and his colleagues at that early time. I had been friendly with Dennis before I had emigrated, and I had much in common with all the staff. Unknown to me, the not being able to sleep was the main indicator of the mood swing syndrome.

Enjoyable early morning bakery visits passed away a few hours and led me up to morning service at church. This was a habit I had adopted most of my life.

In my hometown the morning service was at 8am so I attended and then went for my breakfast. During this holiday there developed a daily routine, bakery, church, home, visiting friends, and then an evening in the pub where a lot of alcohol was consumed.

One morning I was in the bakery and suddenly felt unwell. I was dizzy and had to go out to get some air. A chap with whom I had worked long ago came along and commented on my being up very early in the morning - it was now around 6am. I explained where I had been, that I felt peculiar, and he immediately invited me back to his house. We were chatting, and his family arrived downstairs for their breakfast and I was invited to sit and eat with them. I am not sure, but I suspect that his wife detected there was something wrong with me; perhaps it was my speech or my coherency.

They were concerned when I said that I would go to church, and as I recall, they did not think it wise for me to go. I attended the service and had to leave as the dizziness overwhelmed me again. When I got outside I felt as though I were going to die. My head span and then stopped, leaving me confused and semiconscious. I thought of my blood pressure and the black outs it had caused in the past. Not to drive was an immediate reaction - I would surely have a crash and kill myself.

My state of mind was altered, my thoughts were hazy, and there was no awareness of what I could or should have done in terms of needing immediate treatment, no sense of danger. I had impulses, which drove me to do things I didn't need. I had no control over these. I found myself going to see the garage that was servicing my car - it was but a short walk, but I hitched a lift with a friend for some unknown reason.

Equally unknown are the events of the rest of the morning - I visited my solicitor and after a while of chatting I asked him for a brandy. He replied that no alcohol was kept on the premises - I retorted how little they did to entertain their customers and then promptly left. I wandered along to my local pub - it was 10am and opening time was not until 10.30. I decided not to wait, but to visit my bank, The Bank of Ireland, in the meantime. Mistakenly, I walked into the Munster and Leinster Bank, asked to see the manager, and somehow was shown into his office.

After a short conversation, I asked him for a brandy - his response was the same as my solicitors: no alcohol on the premises. Again I repeated my retort. My next port of call was a grocery shop nearby, the owner of which I knew quite well. I started to throw tomatoes at the clock - customers pretended not to notice - I left. My own family home was close by and was being rented by tenants.

As I had time to kill until opening time, I paid my tenants a visit, a young married couple that I had visited earlier that week. I was chatting with the lady of the house about refurbishing the place. She was a very pleasant woman and we were having a good conversation. Suddenly, and for no apparent reason, I hurled a milk bottle through the sitting room window. I cannot remember this, nor what happened next, but I was outside on the pavement, wandering along when a police car pulled up alongside me and from within the policeman asked me to sit down inside. He drove me to the police station where they questioned me about who I was, etc - I replied I was a former resident of the town and was on holiday there.

I told them how my uncle had joined the police force at its inauguration, and how he had become a sergeant in the force. I also mentioned that my uncle in law had been a sergeant and that he had once been stationed here. At this point, haziness overwhelmed me again -I seemed to be slipping in and out of consciousness. The police produced maps of the town and locality and questioned me on them. I am not sure, but I seem to recall they played some tapes. Then I got the idea I was being interviewed for the Eamon Andrews television show. I was then put in a cell, which seemed dirty and grubby and I offered no resistance or argument at any stage.

I fell asleep and an hour or two must have passed when a policeman appeared at the gate of the cell and enquired if I wanted anything. I replied' a glass of brandy and a doctor - in that order'. I was semi conscious and unsure of what and where I was. I was removed from the cell into a room and a doctor appeared. It was all very strange. The doctor had been my GP prior to my departure to England; he talked to me and suggested that I should go to the hospital in Cork. I agreed; I was prepared to do anything he thought best.

He left and I could hear footsteps echoing along a corridor - suddenly things seemed dramatic. The footsteps belonged to my brother, whom I discovered some time later, had been asked to identify me. His displeasure was apparent and I cannot recall our conversation. My next recollection is that of being driven in an unmarked car to Cork. It was a thirty-mile journey and throughout, I had an idea that I was going to be on the Eamon Andrews Show. I was confused as to whether I was in Ireland or England and when I needed to go to the toilet I was accompanied by three policemen.

We eventually arrived at a hospital and I was taken to a room and left there alone. Then I was convinced that I was dying or had indeed died. I looked around me and saw bells on the walls. I decided to ring them all to see what would happen - apparently I rang every bell in the hospital. A man in a white coat appeared, sat down and started to ask me questions. I thought I had arrived at the pearly gates. Then I thought he was going to give me a new identity and this meant that I was going to be sent back to earth as someone else. I cannot recall anything of this interview.

My next recollection is that of waking up in a ward and weakly trying to get out of bed. Nurses put me back and gave me a sedative. I did not wake up again until the next day and I felt more or less OK. I could remember something of what had happened but I could not understand the cause.

Later I found out the exact cause of the trouble and in so doing, will draw an analogy with a situation following the heart attack, which I suffered eighteen years later. The analogy is to do with Lithium withdrawal. There I was back in hospital, in Cork, and on the second day I was allowed to get up and walk around the grounds. I felt good even though I knew there would be recriminations surrounding my misadventures. I did not see anyone; officially the nurses and patients filled me in as to what had happened. Therapy was on offer and there was a pitch and putt course in the hospital grounds, which patients could use.

My brother and his wife visited me on this second day and I was subjected to a fair amount of criticism in relation to my behaviour. I was told that I should feel ashamed and that I was in an alcoholism ward, which meant that I was one. I remained largely silent and thought to myself 'this is really cheering me up no end'. I think it was also on this day that I got to see the doctor for the first time. We conversed for a while and I found her easy to talk to. She suggested that I should stay in hospital for a while and that I could go into town if I wanted to, but that no alcohol should be consumed.

I told her how I worried that my brother had sectioned me and that I would have wanted someone else to do that on my behalf. She reassured me and said that I should not worry about that. I should explain that a section order is imposed by a wife, husband or near relative when a person will not go into a mental hospital voluntarily. A section order can be for a month, six months or a year. The length of the term could be reduced by good behaviour. This explains my worry - I did not want this to have been determined by my brother. If I had been thinking straight I would have agreed with the doctor to go to the hospital voluntarily -

this was my recollection, but I felt confused. The next day a woman called to see me - a complete stranger - she announced that my sister was outside and wanted to see me if I was agreeable.

Diplomatic relations with both my sister and brother had been severed at different times and I was not on friendly terms with either at this stage. I agreed to see her. I may be many things but I am not bitter. When she entered the room, I guess there was emotion on both sides - certainly there was on my part. We chatted and it was OK; no mention was made of the last few days' events. I appreciated that, as I had to come to terms with it. She invited me to have a meal with the family the next day, Sunday; I was delighted to accept the unexpected invitation.

I received a visit from a cousin that evening. When I told him about the pitch and putt course he said he would bring along a couple of clubs for the following evening. That next day my brother and his children came to visit and whilst it was pleasant to see the children, I had to endure my brother's sarcasm. We went down town as I wanted to buy the children presents. I probably spent what money I had as it gave me much pleasure to treat my nieces and nephews.

When I returned to hospital I realised I had spent every penny I possessed and asked my brother if he would cash a cheque for me. He replied that he had no cash, but when we had been out shopping I had noticed a wad of notes in his pocket. I was inwardly upset, but passed no remark in front of the children. That was the last visit I received from my brother during the rest of my stay in hospital. His absence was a relief - every time I saw him I became upset.

I telephoned my sister and said that I would not be coming to eat with them the next day. She commented that I seemed disturbed and asked me what was wrong. I would not tell her and mumbled words that suggested everyone thought the worst of me. I put the phone down and immediately knew I was in the wrong. An hour later, feeling more composed, I telephoned her to apologise and explained what had happened. She advised me not to worry about my brother's behaviour, that her husband would collect me the following day and that he would cash a cheque for me for whatever amount I needed. He duly arrived, exchanged cash for cheque, and the pleasantness of the day wiped out the bad experience of the previous one.

My stay in hospital had lasted three weeks and I was enjoying it - it seemed almost like a hotel. We were playing pitch and putt most days and on other days I went into Cork. I did not drink any alcohol as I had been ordered by the doctor not to. Despite being in a ward for alcoholics I could honestly say I did not consider myself to be one. The Alcoholics Anonymous for Cork held their meetings in the hospital on a regular basis, and some of the chaps in my ward attended these. I helped to get the refreshments ready for these meetings, which consisted of a couple of dozen people, men and women from all classes of society. I was very impressed by the way they offered help in both advice and anything material that the alcoholic patients needed. There appeared to be a special bond between them. Another thing I noted was that social class made no noticeable difference - there was a family like atmosphere.

The time spent in hospital did not drag - my cousin who had brought the golf clubs visited me nearly every night and I had other visitors as well. Near the hospital was an old asylum, quite a large and formidable building. It had a reputation for being the end of the line; it was for really bad cases of mental illness. I went there and visited a section where they manufactured shoes and ended up buying a pair. An elderly gentleman was in charge of the workshop and I had a very engaging conversation with him. The patients working in the shoe section appeared institutionalised and were, no doubt, long-stay patients.

I knew that an acquaintance from my hometown was a patient and I inquired if I might see him. They said it would be OK to meet, which we did, and had a very pleasant conversation together. Apart from the fact that he had aged, he remained the very nice person that I had known many years ago. I asked him if he ever thought of leaving and he replied that he was happy where he was. Towards the end of my second week in hospital, I was sent to St Finbarr's Hospital for a brain scan, the result of which I was never told.

Seemingly, this trait of withholding information had rubbed off in Ireland as well. In all, I spent about three weeks in hospital and was then released. Notice came for me that I was to be discharged, from a nurse, and at no time was I told what had been wrong with me. This was a continuing pattern of my treatment for each and every hospital I had been a patient in. This retention of information worries me still, but maybe there is a valid explanation. If so, why not inform the patient that the information is confidential to protect the patient, and is therefore for the medical profession only? or something to that effect.

About this time we were beginning to enter the information era, so why stifle it? I decided to go back to my own hometown, maybe because I had to prove a point or two - I was neither a nut case nor an alcoholic. Or it might be that I had been happy with myself in that I had for once been hospitalised without depression being the cause. I knew I was not an alcoholic, but would have preferred to be labelled anything other than that of a dammed depressive.

Upon reaching my hometown I booked into a hotel. I did not want to trouble my good friends whom I had been staying with prior to going into hospital. I felt I might have embarrassed them by my behaviour and what had happened. Besides, I knew the couple that owned the hotel and felt very much at home there. During my stay there, I ate with them and sometimes did so in the privacy of their living quarters. It felt like home from home.

I telephoned Unigate, and told them that I would take another two weeks sick leave to convalesce if they permitted that. They replied that it was fine, all they wished for was my recovery and to return to work fit and well. My colleagues would cover my work, the done thing when anybody was missing, and you returned the good will when your turn came. They jokingly added that I would owe them a few pints of beer upon my return. They asked for the telephone number of the hotel and for me to keep in touch.

I was annoyed with myself and the response to the episode that had taken place - it was difficult to explain to people what had happened to me - in a small town, one step off the kerb is known to all. During those times it was worse, as it was before the advent of television, world communication etc. This left plenty of room for local gossip, and after my behaviour I imagined I was the main topic of conversation. I tried to forget about it and to not let it bother me. It is difficult to describe my mood, a strange combination of being happy and confident, the exact opposite to being depressed, and yet with traces of anger.

One evening in a pub a friend of mine called me to one side and said "I have the greatest admiration for you. You came back to face the music and all the talk surrounding you. Talk is cheap, both you and I know that, you don't have to answer to anyone for what happened." He mentioned that a mutual friend, a reputable businessman, had suffered from a drinking problem a few years ago. He got the notion that dogs were taking over the town and was acting in a very peculiar and abnormal fashion. He went away for treatment and returned to his home within a few weeks; he has been OK every since. The talk at the time of his mishap was irrational, but when people realised the cause they had the greatest admiration for him. My friend ended by saying "I hope you do not mind me mentioning this, it is just that I have always had the highest opinion of you." I thanked him for his remarks but thought inwardly, 'was there a direct correlation to the way in which I had behaved?'

I was not sure if I was being brave, trying to make a point, or whether there happened to be some sort of hidden energy giving me supreme confidence. I certainly felt on terrific form - of course now I know I was on a high, but luckily it was a moderate one. It's like a false kind of euphoria, maybe bordering on ecstasy. The following days I enjoyed myself, and upon encountering people there appeared to be no repercussions from my previous escapade when I was arrested.

I must say that the evenings offered a host of social events with dancing in the hotel almost every evening. One night I went on stage and sang - my spirits were high and it had nothing to do with alcohol. It was just that feeling of being in a great mood, nothing can go wrong, but of course I was ignorant of where this chemistry was coming from - I was on a roll. It is a shame in retrospect that for so many years I did not understand what was happening inside me, perhaps I would have experienced it differently.

One evening, the owner of the hotel asked me if I would like to accompany them to hear Marianne Faithfull sing. This was a wonderful invitation as I was a great fan of hers and I had an interest in her mental state as I knew that she had suffered, had attempted one if not more suicides, and marred her career by drug taking, etc. I gladly went with them, and a cavalcade of cars followed the singer to the hall where she was to perform. I felt genuinely privileged that I was to be their guest at this performance.

After the show, back at the hotel, I had a pleasant chat with Marianne. The following days passed enjoyably - friends came to visit and entertained me by taking me for drives to different places. I telephoned my office and told my colleagues that I would be back at work in a week's time. They were pleased at my progress and hoped I would have made a complete recovery by the time I returned. It was a chance in a million that I had happened along such a fantastic bunch of colleagues such as mine. I spent the rest of my holiday quietly, trying to gather my thoughts and myself together. During that quiet time the feeling of elation dissipated - I was coming down from a high but did not know it.

Before I left Ireland I called to see my sister. My family had a lot of difficulty in understanding that I was suffering from a mental illness, a definite but undefined deficiency. None of us understood the problem or problems; at the very least I hoped that they could try to acknowledge there were reasons beyond my control that affected my mental health and balance. I did no harm to anyone physically; I reserved that for myself. I came back to England and upon my return to work, my colleagues were determined to welcome me and to make things as easy as possible for me. A few weeks later and I felt that normal life had resumed, if there could ever have been any sense of normality in my case.

In 1994 I went to Ireland again to convalesce after my heart attack. Dennis drove me to the airport, my good friend. The flight was delayed for a couple of hours; this was exasperating, especially to a mood swinger. Eventually we got away and the trip was fine, except that when we got close to Cork airport we could not land because of fog. Nearly an hour elapsed before we landed. My sister picked me up and we drove to her house. I did feel a dart of pain in my arm but thought that it had been caused by the way I had been sitting in the plane. Everything was fine and I must say that my sister wanted to give me the best of everything. I had a little walk to the pub every day, and had four half pints of beer. One day I took a pint, but up until then I could not have lifted a pint due to the tremors in my hand.

I had been staying two weeks with my sister and her family and had been enjoying my time with them. The pain in my right side reoccurred and I decided that if it happened again I should see a doctor. My niece came to collect me and drove me to Kinsale, and this is where the tricky part comes in. I was not on the best of terms with my brother. My niece assured me she had explained all about manic depression to him and, if he did not behave properly, she would sort him out.

Our initial meeting went off very well. That evening my brother and his family went for a drink with me - this consisted of my niece and her two brothers. I was on good form, and was cracking jokes one after the other. Everyone, including my brother, was in fits of laughter. We all had a jolly evening, and also it made me proud to be with my niece and nephew. I managed to cover up my arthritis and pseudo-Parkinson's Disease, which were affecting me.

The next day I was a little disappointed when I went for a walk to see the harbour - nobody wanted to accompany me. I could sense a few jibes coming at me from my brother. For instance, my niece got toothpaste or dental cream for my teeth. He remarked 'How many more things are going to be wrong with you?' I did not go out that night, and went to bed early. The next day was Saturday and I went to visit some friends. When I returned that evening I asked my brother if I could make a phone call to Dublin. Then he erupted, saying 'I know you; you will be on the phone all night. The price of phone calls now is very expensive.' I replied, 'Do not worry; I will make the phone call another time. (By the way, a phone call at that particular time actually would have cost 20p for 15 minutes).

My brother must have had a chat with my nephew as he came back and said, 'You can make that call, I am off to church.' I was stunned and humiliated. I would not use that telephone even if my life depended upon it. My brother returned from church and asked if I had made the phone call. I replied that I could not obtain a reply. All night I agonised about that phone call. I could not understand anyone being so mean. If anyone had come to my house and wanted to use the phone, I would have been only too pleased to let him or her use it.

The next day I went to church and then visited some friends. After lunch, I asked my niece to drive me back to Cork. I apologised for not being able to stay; I felt that the environment was not good for me. I could see and feel now that a high I had been suppressing was about to explode.

I do not know why, but my brother accompanied us on this journey. I never spoke to him during it and nor did he to me. I wanted to get as far away from him as I could. When we arrived at my sister's house, my nephew was there alone. My niece dropped me off and went back to her home. I was certainly glad to be out of my brother's company. I explained to my nephew what had happened which made me feel embarrassed, two adults behaving in this manner is despicable. My sister and her husband arrived and there were more explanations. I was unhappy the whole of the following week - I suppose my illness made me vulnerable to any upset. It was clear now to me that I should have stayed in England. What I needed was a nice peaceful convalescence instead of all the aggravation I had been getting.

Towards the end of the week, as my brother-in-law was having a drink with me in a pub, he said, 'Your trouble is that you talk too much about yourself'. This hit me like a ton of bricks. Maybe another time I may not have taken any notice. Certainly it was not the right choice of words at this particular time. I made no comment, and when we went back to his home I made no reference to it. The next couple of days saw me in turmoil. The grand finale came on a Monday morning. I came downstairs for my breakfast, and my sister said both father and son had overslept and been late for work. I casually replied, 'I thought I was the only imbecile around here!'

With that, she lost control of herself and hurled abuse at me; there was no way of trying to reason with her. I told her what her husband had said to me in the pub and that I did not deserve that. I was going to Middleton that day to see a friend. I asked her if she wanted me to return to her home or not. Her reply was that I should suit myself. I took off for Middleton on the bus, disturbed and disgusted. When I arrived, I met my friend Bridget and was able to get a load off my chest. I decided to stay in Middleton that night and asked Bridget to phone my sister to let her know.

The next morning, after attending church, I had a few words with the priest. He did not seem very interested in my tale, and I felt disappointed at his attitude. I was trying to get a neutral opinion about my attitude and personality. It was important to me to know whether I was behaving rationally.

My next visit was to a doctor, as my sister was insisting that I see one. I do not know what miracle she expected from this. After six weeks in hospital with doctors, consultants and psychiatrists, what was a GP in Ireland going to find? You could say that I had been having doctors for breakfast - they had surrounded me. To please her, I was going to attend the first one I came across. The doctor examined me and I recounted to him all of my illness. He advised me to take things very easy. He said that I should stop moving from place to place as I had been. Otherwise, he said, I would have another heart attack.

Before I left I asked could I have a certificate to prove that I had been there. He asked who wanted this certificate or what was it for. I told him it was for my sister, as she would not believe I had seen a doctor. He remarked what a peculiar woman she must be and gave me the certificate.

I am not quite sure what happened next, but I think it was my shaving kit arriving in the post, having been sent by my sister. Because there was no note with it, this upset me. I decided to stay in Middleton for another few days; maybe the whole atmosphere would have defused by then. I wrote a pleasant letter to my sister and brother in law explaining the mood that I was in and that this was in no way disrespectful to them. I spoke to my niece in Kinsale and, unfortunately, came across pretty strongly about her father's attitude. This upset her and from then on I could not get in touch with her. I could not blame her, but she had been the one who had been instrumental in my having come to Ireland. What a mess. I could have been in a convalescent home in Hastings in pleasant and convivial surroundings. My luck certainly was on a downward spiral.

Thank goodness for parks and rivers. I spent the next couple of days meditating in the park. I always derive consolation from watching a river flow by. I tried to figure out what I would do next. Maybe I should go back to England, and then I thought that I might go to Dublin and Dundalk. I had an unconfirmed arrangement with a friend in Dundalk, Kay. She said that she would come to Cork to collect me and then take me back. I could not get in touch with her and she did not telephone me. I learned much later that she had rung and left the message that she would not be coming - a message I never received.

I decided to visit my hometown, Clonakilty; maybe my luck would change. I had another trauma yet to go through - I had to collect my clothes from my sister's home. I asked Bridget to phone my sister and make arrangements on my behalf. Bridget drove me to Cork the next day, and I collected my clothes. They had been neatly ironed and arranged for my collection. To my surprise, there was no one in the house and I found this hard to understand; it was evident they did not want to see me. I went back to Middleton by bus, as Bridget had to attend a meeting.

I was in a state and now none of my family wanted to talk to me. I was not in the best of health either physically or mentally. For the first time in ages, my mood was fluctuating up and down and I had no way of controlling it. A 'normal' person would have found all these family politics stressful. I kept saying to myself, 'do not let this situation get you down.' It was now evident that my family could never understand or accept my mood swings. Even though it hurts, it is better to know the truth. I decided to spend two more days in Middleton, and then headed for my hometown. Probably Bridget would be getting fed up with the carry on.

I was lucky I got a lift most of the way to my hometown. I booked into a hotel and somehow felt relieved that a whole lot of trouble was behind me. That evening, I met up with a few old friends and had a few drinks. I restricted myself to four half pints - quite an achievement in Ireland. I think that people don't pour drinks into you once they know that you have a health problem. I guess the talk and nostalgia made a very pleasant evening.

The next day I met a very good friend and inquired from him who would be the best doctor to visit. He recommended me to one and I went along to see him in the afternoon. I wanted to check on my mental state again, in case there might be something I was missing.

It was good that I had come to this particular doctor: he was as good as any psychiatrist I had seen and knew straight away that I was quite stressed.

I explained to him the happenings for the last couple of months. He said that a lot of the stress had been caused by the lack of lithium in my system. It would take a time for what I was taking now to take effect. All this was due to the time in hospital when I had been taken off it. He said for me not to get stressed, to try to take things easy; he would see me again the next day. I felt very relieved after seeing him.

That evening I had a few drinks with friends and I was much more relaxed. The next day I visited the doctor, and upon seeing me he commented that I was a different person to the one he had seen the previous day. 'You are calm and composed a complete contrast to how you were yesterday. Your sister has been on the phone wanting to know about you - I sent her away with a flea in her ear. She should have known better, it would be unethical of any doctor to disclose information about a patient.' The doctor's attitude was having a good effect upon me; we had a long chat and he said that if I needed him to give him a call.

The next day I met up with another good friend, Matt Sullivan. Matt was to drive me to many different places over the next few days. That evening I did not feel well and went back to the hotel early. As I was walking along the street I could feel pain in my right arm and side. I had to stop half a dozen times to rest. That night I was in terrible pain and felt like calling the doctor, but I survived until the morning. I went to see the doctor very early, as I was very apprehensive about the pain. He diagnosed that I had angina, which was an after-affect of my heart attack. I was to take things easy and was given tablets to put under my tongue, which reduced the pain.

It was only now I discovered that where I was staying and where I was socialising was too great a distance for me to walk. I felt old and restricted, even though it was a temporary condition. Then I found that people were only too willing to give me a lift wherever I needed to go. Matt Sullivan took me in his car to different places and this coincided with his work. It was great fun for me, as I had not seen some of these places for over 30 years.

There was a letter for me at the hotel from my sister. I telephoned her and said that there was no animosity on my part. I told her that I would come back in a couple of days to see them. I did go back, but I found it a very strained atmosphere. I decided that I would be better off away from there. One night, I visited some good friends as I was feeling down and fed up, and worried as to what would be the right thing to do. At first, I decided to just leave quietly, and then I decided that I would tell her I was expecting mail to arrive from England at the hotel I had been staying in Clonakilty and this meant that I had to return there. I had to also visit my doctor there to follow up treatment. My friends were fabulous, and that helped me make the decision - they were very supportive and understanding.

The next day I fold my sister my plans and that I would be going away the next day. The atmosphere was awful and I could not wait to leave. That night I went to the pub but could not drink, as I had had my quota of two pints during the day. I had two half pints, this took me to 9pm. I did not want to go back to my sisters until everyone was in bed. I was left with only one option - to walk the streets for a couple of hours. If ever I did some straight thinking it was then. What a mess I had got myself into. I should have stayed in England in a nursing home. On the other hand, I had found out once and for all where I stood with my brother and sister. It was a miserable, painful way to find out, but from now on I would be under no misapprehension or illusion. It made me sad that my family could not replicate the wonderful understanding I had from my friends. My own family treated me as if I were some mentally retarded creature. It was no consolation to me when doctors told me that some families could not accept that mental maladies were an illness like any other.

I decided that from that time on I would never be in their company again. The next morning, my friend collected me and took me to Clonakilty. Thank goodness I had a few peaceful days more at ease with myself. Matt Sullivan came and collected me and took me for some lovely drives. I was a little perturbed that my friends in Dublin and Dundalk had not contacted me, but I decided I mustn't worry over that either. A couple of days later I was on my way back to England. My friends drove me to Cork airport. It surprised me when I found my sister and her husband there to wish me farewell. I treated them reservedly and could not wait to board the plane. I found it very hard to forget about what had happened in Ireland upon my return to England. I felt in worse shape than I had before I left.

15. Observations and Feelings

It is sad that more money is not made available for research into mental health. Doctors tell me that I have a chemical imbalance in the brain. To a degree it can be controlled, but not cured.

Changes were happening, gradual but discernible. It is always difficult to explain deep despair; it is by the same token difficult to explain coming out of it. Those who do not suffer are completely puzzled by it; whilst at the same time recognise cancer as a chronic disease. That is partly due to cancer being physical, yet mental troubles are classified as illness and could be termed as a cancer of the mind. Perhaps the greatest help to those who suffer from mental illness is others' understanding of it.

All the myths and misrepresentations surrounding it will have to go, before such understanding can be arrived at. I digress here to illustrate how, in my own case, it took such a long time to achieve some sort of recovery. Also, there was no particular reason for my illness to begin with. For whatever reasons, I am feeling better and have not felt like this for a long time.

People sometimes say, "Give yourself a good shake". They mean well, but all mood swingers hate the phrase. I do not think that I would have been kept in hospital for some signs of a whimsy of a depression. Even though you try to tell yourself it will not last, it is impossible to convince yourself of this. Confidence plummets when I put myself down and I think that everyone else is seeing me from my own eyes. These circumstances make me withdrawn and not want to be in the company of others.

When I am well or unwell, work and play is the same environment. Yet when I am unwell, the smallest of problems takes on a major proportion. The simplest of tasks scares me. When the day's work is finished a huge sense of relief comes. Stupid obsessively scrupulous thoughts harass me, like 'have I completed this task correctly' at work.

Arriving home from work, I cannot eat. I sit there hoping that the thing will go away but there I remain in a black sea of lonely despair. I cannot go out and I dread conversation because I will have nothing to contribute. This leads to the inevitable comment of 'you are very quiet tonight'. This makes me feel worse, and I wish something would come and make me disappear.

Society does not look at mental illness as an illness like any other physical illness, nor does it give those who experience it the credit of the bravery of the struggle to recover. At that time, I had just one friend I could fully confide in, Eamon. He seemed like a guardian angel to me. Other friends were most helpful, but were hesitant as to what was wrong with me. I did not know this either. I was still not a whole person in real life and my confidence was sorely lacking.

It is difficult to describe how feeling low is - I could use the analogy of the boxer who has been knocked to the floor. Winded and concussed, it is so difficult to get up. Maybe the boxer can rise very slowly, the commentator loudly says, 'he is up on one knee'. This gives an indication he can still win the fight. I am always at the one knee stage!

All through my life I have been attracted to slogans and parables. I think and believe that Our Lord spoke in parables, therefore how infinitely good they must be. One saying I often repeat to myself, especially when the going gets tough, is 'The glory is not in never falling, but in rising every time we fall'. In the months that followed, I slowly improved.

There had been a misunderstanding between my Uncle Michael and myself concerning collecting a cousin from Heathrow Airport. This became a disproportionate issue and amazingly, I did not fall out with my Uncle then or at any other time. Apart from being my Uncle, he was too nice a person to contemplate being at loggerheads with. However, the accumulation of pain, lack of sleep, and this slight tension with my Uncle were all getting to me. Something happened during this time, which was to prove very significant in later years.

I had to contend with the idea that I might never work again - this was a soul-destroying prospect. Sometimes I felt guilty when relaxing; I felt that I should be doing something. This reminds me of the times when I was high - for example, I would polish the furniture in the sitting room, then I would move on into the dining room; I would go all around the house into every room I could and could not stop myself working. This also applies to talking; I would walk up to complete strangers and could not stop talking to them.

It is a shame that I have rheumatoid arthritis, as both illnesses interact at times, and, the arthritis can itself be very depressing.

I suppose I think the same mixture of thoughts as each New Year comes; it is now seventeen years since I have been in a mental hospital. Maybe I have had a lot of help along the way, but I have also put in a great effort myself to try to keep a handle on my condition. Mood swings is an illness that sometimes cannot be controlled, and like any physical illness it has to be accepted. It makes me so sad that my brother and sister cannot understand the condition.

The contrast hurts even more - my friends understand and give me their support, and yet it is not given to those of my own flesh and blood. As I have mentioned, the Open University has become my surrogate family. It has supported me therapeutically for a long time and helped to contain my mood swings and my forbearance on the arthritis. At least the knowledge I have gained helps me to deal with both illnesses better.

I sometimes think that 'normal' people do not understand the handicap and frustrations that a mood swinger is subjected to. When applying for jobs, I could never disclose that I was a manic-depressive. If I had, I would not have got the job. Then I had to wrestle with my conscience, and satisfy myself this omission was the right thing to do. In all groups and discussions, whether or not to reveal all is a grey area. It is more or less left to the individual to decide what works for him or her.

On getting a job, if I fell ill, usually my GP gave me a medical certificate for nervous exhaustion. Should any of my colleagues at work have found out that I suffered from mood swings or some form of mental illness, they might become apprehensive. For instance, I have a crisis card that is issued to me by The Fellowship. This is an excellent form of referral because it gives details, name, medication and doctor's name, in case one gets into a bad situation. The irony of this was I was afraid to carry it with me when working. The worry for me was that I might pull it out of my wallet by mistake and someone might see it.

It might seem that I am very preoccupied with myself. Ask any mood swinger and they will tell you a similar story. What then is the answer to our problem? The ideal scenario would be to have people in general better informed about the nature of the illness. This would be a major undertaking, but a start should be made. Some kind of initiative would have to be taken by the World Health Organisation or by the UK government. I feel that an understanding by the general public would be a better cure than tablets.

In those days, people could not differentiate between the different categories of mental health. Mood swings rarely featured in the news or in the media. Consequently, when there was mention of mental illness by the media, there was certain apathy about it. I felt embarrassed and guilty, and also feared discrimination when it was mentioned. Some people's reaction was 'oh! it is one of them again.' This conveyed to me the discrimination element of 'them and us'. I would add that it is not probably intentional but it does hurt.

There are many times in my everyday life when I am reminded that I am a mood swinger. Yet I believe myself that most of the time I am just the same human being that everyone else is. I have been trying to indicate the pitfalls and way of life for one with mood swings. I have also suggested remedies and ways that might alleviate the suffering and help create a more whole way of living. It is not any special treatment or any favours. I am asking for a little understanding and for those with mental illness to not be discriminated against.

I am sure there will be a time when others will gain the understanding that they need. Then we, the affected, can take our place in society without feelings of alienation. A greater understanding from the general public would improve immensely the life of sufferers and their carers. I think that the general public would accept knowledge and education if they could be given to them. Ignorance is a major obstacle to the acceptance of the illness. In America the attitude to mental health is very different. It is even fashionable to visit a psychiatrist (an analyst).

If by some stroke of fortune this book is published, I will donate any revenue to worthwhile causes. I have been lucky, and Eamon Coyne and Denis Treacy have looked out for me. The Open University has been a home for me. Maybe one day the nasty illness, which I call mood swings will leave me forever.

16. Epilogue

At the end of writing "Why Me" My greatest hope was that this illness would one day depart from me forever. How deeply was that hope felt and expressed, how cruelly has it not been fulfilled. Just last summer, 1999, I was attacked by an overwhelming bout of depression, which left me dumbfounded and sad - my confidence and concentration were shattered by its onslaught and it took some months to relinquish its grip upon me.

Then the real downside struck - an almighty high (mania) hit me in a way that I had never experienced before.

I was the victim of all of the attacks wrought by this possessive mania ...I was out of my mind, I argued about trivial matters at great lengths with my friends and family... I went on a mad shopping spree and spent lots of money...

Throughout these periods of excess, which apparently lasted for two months, the seriousness of my condition was unknown to me. It was unaffected by lithium, the drug I habitually take to stabilise my illness, and worst of all, unrecognised by many friends and family who had not experienced a mania of this magnitude before. Such manifestation of a high had not occurred within a time span of twenty-five years.

I was finally hospitalised after seeing my GP and for the first time I was sectioned for a six-month period - this section would remain in place at the discretion of the consultants under whom I was placed responsible. The hospitalisation was further, and unnecessarily, confusing for my friends - I had requested that no information be given to anyone who enquired. This was a maniacal tactic to protect myself, and the hospital staff adhered to my request, thus preventing friends and family from receiving any information as to my condition.

It was, singularly, the worst period of my recent life. I was finally able to leave hospital after six weeks on the condition that I attended the day centre four times a week - this was to ensure that the inevitable 'down' that would follow the 'high' could be monitored and treated. My thanks to the National Health Service for the treatment philosophy and aftercare policy that now exists in the year 2000 for my illness. My attendance at the day centre was reduced to two days a week after a further period of six weeks observation.

The other difficult outcome lies in the lack of knowledge that I have about the 'high' that I have experienced. How to come to terms with this has made me feel profoundly depressed, and doubly so as I am feeling shattered by the experience itself.

It has proved to me that I will never be able to control the impact of this illness, never be prepared for its next attack, and never able to repair fully the damage it wreaks.

This epilogue is the only part of 'Why Me?' that I would have preferred to not have had to write.

London, September 2000

THE END